Wilma Tenderfoot

and the case of
the Rascal's Revenge

Emma Kennedy writes things for the radio and
the tellybox. She also does some dressing up and
pretending to be other people on TV. Sometimes
she wins prizes for these things, but her greatest
achievement EVER was being the Runner-Up World
Conker Champion. She would have won, but was let
down by a soft nut. There are two things she would
like to do before she dies. 1. She would like to fly a
hot-air balloon. Proper fly it, not just stare out of it
like a lemon. And 2. Grow wings. That's it. She has a
most excellent beagle called Poppy, who can walk like
a crab. Emma's favourite word is ramalamadingdong.

Wilma Tenderfoot and the Case of the Frozen Hearts
was shortlisted for the Hull Children's Book Award,
the Gateshead Children's Book Award
and the Southwark Book Award.

Theodore P. Goodman's Ten Top Tips For Detecting

1. Contemplate the clues.
2. Make deductions based on those clues.
3. Keep a sharp lookout for suspects and sometimes creep around after them.
4. Eavesdropping, while not encouraged in polite society, will often produce results.
5. When escaping, be circuitous.
6. Always write things down.
7. Using a disguise can sometimes be cunning (especially when things have gone a bit precarious).
8. Proper detectives always save what they're thinking till last.
9. Behave seriously at all times.
10. Never go detecting on an empty stomach.

Emma Kennedy

Wilma Tenderfoot

and the case of
the Rascal's Revenge

Illustrated by Tom Morgan-Jones

MACMILLAN CHILDREN'S BOOKS

First published 2011 by Macmillan Children's Books
a division of Macmillan Publishers Limited
20 New Wharf Road, London N1 9RR
Basingstoke and Oxford
Associated companies throughout the world
www.panmacmillan.com

ISBN 978-0-330-53523-6

Printe

Th
b
or
i
it i

For Dawn French, who made me
want to be funny in the first place

Firstly thank you to Alex Todd, Louise Cope and Daniel
Chapman, who all came to my aid on Twitter when I
couldn't remember words; secondly to my tremendous agent
Sheila Crowley at Curtis Brown, who stops me floundering
like a just-caught fish; thirdly to Emma, Richard, Scarly,
Jake, Charlie and Spike, who let me stay in their house and
get this book finished, and lastly but oh not so very leastly
to Ruth Alltimes and Samantha Swinnerton at
Macmillan, who consistently make me better
than I could ever be.
Without you all I
am nothing.

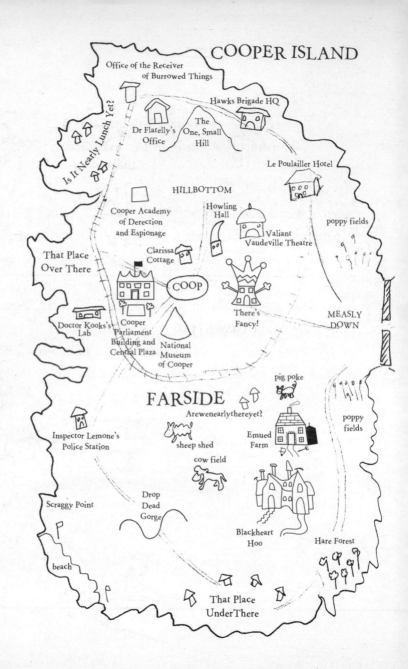

COOPER ISLAND

Office of the Receiver
of Burrowed Things

Hawks Brigade HQ

Is It Nearly Lunch Yet?

Dr Flatelly's
Office

The
One, Small
Hill

Le Poulailler Hotel

HILLBOTTOM

Cooper Academy
of Derection
and Espionage

Howling
Hall

poppy fields

Clarissa
Cottage

Valiant
Vaudeville Theatre

That Place
Over There

COOP

There's
Fancy!

MEASLY
DOWN

Doctor Kooks's
Lab

Cooper
Parliament
Building and
Central Plaza

National
Museum
of Cooper

pig poke

FARSIDE

Arewenearlythereyet?

poppy
fields

sheep shed

Emued
Farm

cow field

Inspector Lemone's
Police Station

Drop
Dead
Gorge

Scraggy Point

Blackheart
Hoo

Hare Forest

beach

That Place
UnderThere

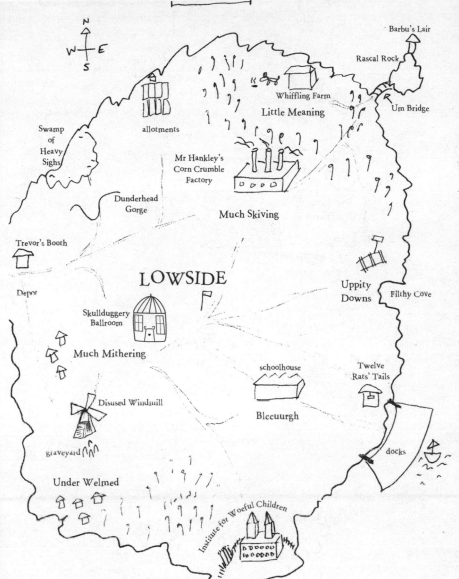

Chapter 1

As dawn's first light broke over the crest of Cooper's One Small Hill, Pickle didn't look good. Wilma pursed her lips and took a long hard stare. Her beagle was swaying gently, his feet tied to springs. Strapped to his back was a set of tea towels stitched on to two wooden spoons. Behind them perched a small saddlebag tied on with a large leather belt and on his head he wore a yellow glove on one ear and a purple sock on the other. He was MORTIFIED.

'I'm not sure you need that beard,' said Wilma, indicating the large hairy whiskers dangling from Pickle's muzzle. 'It might get in the way. What with us having to do the Salt Course and everything.'

'Assault Course,' corrected Kite Lambard, headmistress of the Cooper Academy of Detection and Espionage, of which Wilma was the sole pupil. 'Not salt. Right then. Are you ready? I'm going to open this door and you're going to go in, locate the secret file and bring it back to me. Think you can do it?'

Wilma pursed her lips and nodded. 'I may be small, Miss Lambard,' she retorted, 'but I'm VERY determined.'

'Super. You've got ten minutes.' And with that Kite gently pushed Wilma and Pickle into the room and closed the door behind them.

'It's pitch black,' said Wilma. 'Can you see anything, Pickle?' But as she spoke they both took a step forward and fell, suddenly, downward.

'Aaaaaaaargh!' screamed Wilma, landing with a thump.

Suddenly there was a hissing sound to the right. Wilma snapped her head in the direction of the noise.

'What was that?' she whispered, startled. Pickle gave a small, low growl from beside her. 'I've got a candle in my pocket. Don't move until I've lit it.' Reaching into her pinafore, Wilma pulled out a long candle and a box of matches. She lit the wick and the candle's glow spread outward into the room. 'Right,' she said, lifting the candle upward. 'Let's see what we're up against . . . 'Aaaaaaaaaaaargh!' Wilma screamed again, shuffling as far back against the wall as she could. 'Snake pit!' she wailed.

Pickle, whose day was getting worse with every passing second, lifted his nose into the air and sniffed. He could smell

2

fresher air, but where was it coming from?

'Hang on,' Wilma said, gingerly pulling a snake from her pinafore pocket, tail first, and flinging it across the room. 'We need to think wonkily. Mr Goodman was once cornered by some snakes. It was during the Case of the Scraped Knee. And, if I remember correctly, he escaped with the help of a chicken!'

Theodore P. Goodman was, of course, Cooper Island's most famous and serious detective. He was Wilma's hero and, rather brilliantly, she now got to work for him every day as his detective's apprentice. There wasn't a single thing about Theodore P. Goodman that Wilma didn't know because over the years she had collected all the newspaper clippings reporting Theodore's incredible, and often dangerous, detective cases. Wilma had attached the articles to a Clue Ring, a sort of key ring clipped to her belt, which she carried with her everywhere.

Wilma clicked her fingers. 'That's it! Cooper snakes have a morbid fear of hens!'

Pickle snorted. That was all very well, but they didn't have a chicken to hand.

'Can you impersonate a chicken, Pickle?' asked Wilma, shooing off an adder sliding up her sleeve. 'You know, do some pecking? Clucking? Flapping? Lay an egg, maybe?'

Pickle stared at his beloved best friend. She'd asked him to do many things in their time together, but he was a noble hound with a reputation to protect and there was NO WAY he was going to pretend to lay an egg.

'Look,' said Wilma, rattling on. 'You can use that yellow glove on your left ear as a coxcomb. If I pull it over your head a bit,' she added, grabbing it and yanking it down over Pickle's forehead, 'and if I put that purple sock over the end of your nose so that it looks a bit like a beak then . . . do you know what? . . . I think you can pull it off.'

Well, this really took the biscuit. Here he was, springs on paws, mouth trussed up in some old sock with a badly knitted yellow glove as a hat. Still, he was now their only chance of not being swallowed alive by pythons and being slowly and painfully digested over a period of up to two months.

'Go on, Pickle, please,' urged Wilma, her gaze never leaving a large python who was eyeing her hungrily. 'It's our only chance!'

With a heavy sigh, Pickle gingerly stepped forward, his springs wobbling erratically.

'Baaaooooo,' he half bayed, adding a cough at the end to try to sound more like a chicken. The snakes, whose circle had been tightening about the intrepid pair, stopped slithering.

Wilma looked about brightly. 'It's working, Pickle! Peck at the floor. Flap your tea towels!'

4

Pickle, encouraged that his brilliant acting was working, jumped bravely towards the horde of snakes while pulling the cord that was hanging from his back with his sock-covered mouth. As he yanked downward, the tea towels, sewn on to the wooden spoons, shot outward and flapped gently, looking for all the world like chicken wings. The snakes nearest him reared up and backwards, hissing with terror.

Pickle was impressed with himself. Could he nail this once and for all and . . . lay an egg? He began to crouch . . .

'Ooooh no, Pickle!' cried out Wilma. 'I haven't got a bag! And, besides, they're all crawling off! Look there! An exit tunnel! Quickly! We've only got five minutes left to finish the training trial!'

The tunnel was thankfully a short one and they soon came out into fresh air.

'We're outdoors,' said Wilma, standing up and dusting down her pinafore. 'That's odd,' she added, looking at the four sheer walls surrounding her. 'We must be somewhere in the middle of the Academy. I didn't know it had a garden. It's very overgrown; I can't see over the grass. So all we have to do now is find the secret file. Come on!'

Wilma set off, hacking away at the tall weeds with a wooden stick. Pickle, just behind her, tried to take a step, but the springs on his paws were so big and heavy he quickly realized all he could do was wobble on the spot.

Wilma stopped and looked back at him. 'Try bouncing a bit,' she whispered. 'Oooh . . . that's given me an idea. Can you bounce any higher, Pickle? So you can see over the grass.'

Easy for her to say, thought Pickle. And why was he wearing springs anyway? No one had explained that to him. NO ONE. He gave a small sigh and, with a quick shimmy of his hindquarters, dropped his shoulders and pressed himself towards the floor. The springs crunched downward beneath him, then, as Pickle released the tension, they exploded. The beagle shot upward at an alarming rate.

'Oh my,' Wilma gasped, as he hurtled past her, out of control.

But when he came back down and the springs compacted into the ground, flinging the beagle skyward again, Wilma caught hold of the tightly secured belt round his middle. Her feet left the ground and upward they sprang.

'Now pull open your wings! There's a bit of breeze. We might be able to float over the garden and see where the secret file is.'

Pickle pulled down on his wing cord and out spread the tea towels, immediately catching the wind. Over the garden they soared, cresting on eddies and floating on gentle gusts.

Wilma, her dirty-blonde pigtails flapping behind her, peered down. She could just make out a clearing at the garden's centre.

'Veer right, Pickle,' she called, pointing towards it.

It isn't often that a small beagle with one tatty ear gets to have a go at paw gliding, but here Pickle was, springs twanging and tea-towel wings engaged. Even he had to admit this wasn't all bad.

The brave beagle shifted his shoulder right and they circled the clearing.

'There's a plinth!' shouted Wilma, her green eyes flashing with excitement. 'And there's something on it. Let's go in for landing!'

Wheeling on the breeze, the pair descended and, as soon as she was near enough to the ground, Wilma let go of Pickle's belt and rolled on to the grass as the small hound crashed into the bush behind her. She picked herself up and scampered towards the plinth.

'We've found it!' she exclaimed, delighted. 'It's the file! I'll just reach up and grab it.'

But as her fingers touched their prize and she lifted it from the plinth, there was a small click.

'Oh no,' whispered Wilma, realizing what she'd done. 'Booby trap . . .' And, before she could do anything more, a large net

7

hidden under the leaves beneath their feet scooped Wilma and Pickle up together towards the main building.

They were trapped.

'Oh, bad luck,' said Kite, her head popping through a hidden shuttered window above them. 'Should have warned you about the booby traps. Standard assault-course procedure, according to the book.'

She waved the handbook of the Academy of Detection and Espionage in the air and grinned before winching the daring duo up through the window. They scrambled out from the net as it was lowered on to the floor.

'Well done and everything,' Kite continued. 'You didn't quite pass the assault-course training, but you gave it a good go. And you did manage the snake pit quite well. I suppose I can give you two lumps for that. There you are,' she added, handing Wilma a couple of sugar cubes.

'Lumps?' asked Wilma, frowning. Pickle licked his lips.

'Oh. Am I not supposed to give lumps?' asked Kite, grabbing the Academy handbook and flicking through it. 'Ah. No. That's for hot drinks. Oh well.'

Wilma blinked. Her headmistress was a little bit hopeless if truth be told, but it didn't stop her liking her.

'Umm, Miss Lambard,' said Wilma, as she untied the springs from Pickle's feet, 'why did we have to do the assault-course

8

training anyway? It's not very detective-like. And I am an Apprentice Detective, after all.'

'Well, here's the thing,' said Kite, clearing her throat and putting her book down. 'This is the Academy of Detection AND Espionage and what with us properly reopening the case to find Max and Pru it's sort of important you understand all about spying. Because Max and Pru were spies. To spy really well you need to be in tip-top physical shape and be able to think quickly to get yourself out of sticky situations.'

Wilma nodded enthusiastically. 'I see,' she said.

Wilma had only just found out about Max and Pru, last week at the conclusion of the Case of the Fatal Phantom, and, to be honest, it had all been a bit overwhelming. Wilma was abandoned as a baby at the gates of the Lowside Institute for Woeful Children, wrapped in a stained butcher's muslin cloth, with nothing to identify who she really was other than a luggage tag tied round her wrist with the words 'Because They Gone' on it. She had wondered all her life where she might have come from. So when Wilma became an Apprentice Detective she was determined to find out who she *really* was and began her own investigation: the Case of the Missing Relatives.

Wilma had been brought up believing she was an orphan, but suddenly, out of the blue, her old orphanage matron, Madam

9

Skratch, had revealed that she had a living relative. Who it was, Wilma did not know, but she had seen letters paying for her monthly upkeep and another letter written by Kite herself who had gone to the institute searching for a child that had been linked to Pru, her sister, and Max, Pru's husband and Theodore's best friend, who had gone missing over ten years ago, just before Wilma was born. Kite and Theodore had searched endlessly for Max and Pru, but it had come to nothing and they'd all but given up hope until just last week, when Kite had found a message in a bottle that had reignited everyone's dreams. It was from Max and it said, '*All is not lost*,' dated two months previously. Max and Pru were still alive! But *where* were they? And what light could they shed on Wilma's own past? They might even be Wilma's parents!

If Max and Pru *were* Wilma's parents, of course, that would make Kite Wilma's aunt, another reason why Wilma tried not to get annoyed about Kite being an exceptionally clueless headmistress. As a general rule, odd behaviour in strangers is totally unacceptable. But when a member of your own family starts talking to trees or communicating ONLY via the medium of dance, it's utterly charming. If in doubt, just smile and nod.

'I suppose I should explain,' said Kite, standing and clasping her hands behind her back. 'I was never meant to be the Headmistress of the Academy of Detection and Espionage. It

was Pru's job. But until I find her I'm sort of standing in. Max and Pru were Cooper's best spooks.'

Wilma frowned. 'They're ghosts?'

Kite laughed. 'No. A spook can be a ghost, yes, but it also means someone who's a spy.'

'Adults are always using words that mean two things at once,' grumbled Wilma quietly to Pickle. 'I'll be honest, it's verging on sneaky.'

'And I suspect that their spooking is what got them into the mess they're in,' continued Kite. 'That means one thing, Wilma.'

Wilma blinked and waited.

'You and I are going to have to become espionage-a-teers!'

'Is that a real word?'

'No. No it isn't.'

Let the adventures commence.

11

Chapter 2

Wilma gazed up at her headmistress dubiously, a bit like when wives have just been told by their husbands that no, it's fine, they don't need to call in a plumber to fix the burst pipe because 'how difficult can it be?'. In short, Wilma wasn't entirely convinced that Kite Lambard was up to the job. All the same, she wanted to be encouraging so she twisted her mouth sideways and said nothing.

'So I think,' said Kite, bending down and rummaging through a box on the floor, 'that I ought to kick things off with Double Surveillance.'

Wilma shook her head. 'What's that?'

'It's when spooks watch people.'

'Don't they just use their eyes?' asked Wilma.

'Yes,' answered Kite, reaching down further into the box. 'But they use other things as well. Secret things. Ah! Here it is.'

She pulled out a thin blue book with a battered cover. 'Academy Espionage Class Planner. First year.' She grinned and gave it a little wave in the air. Opening it, she scanned the contents page. 'Codes. No. Secret panels — that's when houses have hidden rooms. We can do that another day. How to kill a man through the nose?' she said, frowning. 'That's for first years? Good grief. Don't think we'll bother with that. Right. Here we are. Surveillance. Chapter Eight . . .' She flicked forward and scanned the pages quickly. 'According to this you have to bug the room. Think you can do that?'

Wilma pursed her lips and raised her eyebrows. 'Ummm . . .'

'Super. Well, you crack on with that and I'll go and take another look at that message in a bottle I found from Max.' And off she marched, waving as she went.

Wilma glanced down at Pickle, who, despite managing to shake off most of his costume, was still wearing his beard. 'Bugging the room, Pickle. Any ideas?'

But Pickle's attention was elsewhere. Of course he didn't have any ideas. He only had eyes for the half-eaten sandwich left sitting on Kite's desk. Looked like it had a bit of ham in it too. Who in their right mind would abandon that? He'd never understand humans.

'What's that thing Mr Goodman always tells me to do when

13

I'm in a brain-fizz?' Wilma asked, scrunching her nose up. 'Think *logically*. So if I have to *bug* the room, then I need to get bugs!'

'Done it, Miss Lambard,' panted Wilma an hour later, as she skidded into the Academy science lab. 'I've bugged the room.'

'Jolly good,' replied Kite, looking up from the microscope she'd been peering into. 'I found a strange substance in that bottle, smeared on the underside of the note. Just having a closer look at it.'

'What is it?'

'Something . . . grey,' answered Kite. 'Very . . . grey.'

Wilma stared but said nothing. While she was pretty sure that there was probably something her headmistress was extremely good at, what that might be remained a mystery. It certainly wasn't teaching or science.

'Perhaps you could ask Penbert to have a look at it. You know. At the proper lab?'

'Ah yes. Good idea,' said Kite, taking off her blue lab coat. 'But let's go and see how you've got on first.'

'Didn't I leave a sandwich in here?' asked Kite, pointing to the empty plate on her desk as they entered. 'No matter . . . now then. Your bugs. I'll try to find them. I expect the main thing is that they're properly hidden.'

Wilma nodded and cast a suspicious eye in Pickle's direction. 'You've got crumbs in your beard,' she whispered, giving him a nudge with her foot.

Pickle tried to look as if he didn't know what she was talking about. But he did. He knew full well. The incriminating evidence was tucked away safely where no one would find it — in his belly.

In many ways, thought the beagle, it was the perfect crime. Apart from the crumbs in the beard.

'Can't see anything round the door,' said Kite, hands on hips as she examined the frame. She turned and smiled at Wilma, and then strode purposefully towards her bureau. 'Nothing on the shelf. Nothing in the lamp. Nothing in the . . . actually, what is that?' she asked, pointing towards something round and brown in her opened box of pencils. 'Oh. It's the apple I started eating last Wednesday.'

Pickle raised his snout expectantly.

'Don't even think about it,' said Wilma, from the corner of her mouth.

Kite pulled back the chair from her desk and sat down. 'Still found nothing. You've done well, Wilma,' she beamed, reaching for the handle of the top drawer. 'Just have a look in here and

15

OH!' she cried, pushing her chair back suddenly. 'OH! That's just . . . OH!'

The inside of Kite's top drawer was a swirling mass of worms, caterpillars and winged beetles that took advantage of the now open drawer to fly upward into Kite's face. The headmistress leaped from her chair and ran around the room, flapping her arms in an attempt to rid herself of the flying insects.

'There you go, Miss Lambard,' Wilma grinned. 'I bugged the room. Now the place is full of them,' she added, pointing at the beetles flying through the air. 'I put some woodlice behind the bookcase. And some ants on the paperweight. There's a few cockroaches sitting on top of the filing cabinet and I found a wasp nest. That's in the other drawer.'

Kite ran back to her desk and lunged quickly at the second drawer handle. Pulling the drawer open, she jumped back to cower behind a curtain. The wasps, enraged at being cooped up, shot out from the drawer like bullets, and dive-bombed through the open window, but not before delivering a few angry stings to Kite as a parting shot.

'Miss Lambard?' asked Wilma, standing over the now collapsed headmistress. 'Are you all right?'

Kite was staring listlessly up at the ceiling, her face a mass of red welts. She was breathing heavily.

'You look excessively startled,' added Wilma. 'Did I pass the bugging test?'

Kite swallowed and sat up. 'Yes,' she panted. 'Let's say you did. Then you don't have to do it again.'

Before Wilma could celebrate, however, the sound of a trumpet being blown rang out grandly from outside. The young apprentice peered out into the street to see an ornately dressed gentleman below blowing on a long horn.

Taking it from his lips, he bellowed, 'Take note, citizens of Cooper! The Ten-Annual Election is upon us! All citizens are required to display a poster!'

Kite pulled herself up and joined Wilma at the window. 'Gosh. Is it ten years already? Run down and fetch a poster, would you, Wilma? And meet me in the sanatorium. I need to . . . smother.'

The Academy for Detection and Espionage was a peculiar box-shaped building that, on the face of it, had no entrance. But, for those in the know, there was a secret front door, set invisibly into the black brick wall, and hidden strategic peepholes that looked out on to the street from the inside rooms. Wilma, who was still the only enrolled pupil, had been gradually working through most of the building's secrets. She'd found the Creeping Cupboard, the Fingerprint Parlour, the Magnifying Mirror and a host of other tucked-away places, but there was still much to be discovered. The best thing she'd worked out, though, was how to open the front door, and scampering down from Kite's office, Pickle at her heel, she ran straight to the stone bust of a detective that sat on a plinth in the main entrance hall. Reaching up she pulled down on the large and pointy nose and – hey presto! – the front door popped open.

'I love doing that,' she grinned.

Running out into the street, Wilma joined the small queue of people who had gathered before the Cooper Crier.

'ONE POSTER PER HOUSEHOLD!' he yelled. 'ALL CITIZENS REQUIRED TO DISPLAY!'

The posters he was handing out were cream-coloured with a luxurious, patterned red border. In the centre of the poster was a picture of a woman's face set into an ornate oval frame. She was wearing a three-piece suit and a monocle, and had her hair short and slicked down.

'SAY FAREWELL TO YOUR COOPERATE GENERAL GLENDA BLAIZE!' the poster read. 'THE TEN-ANNUAL ELECTION IS UPON US. THREE GRAND CEREMONIES OVER THREE DAYS, STARTING TONIGHT! EVERY CITIZEN REQUIRED TO ATTEND!'

'Can I have a poster, please?' asked Wilma politely, as she reached the Cooper Crier. He was a rotund fellow with a mouth that was way too small for the rest of his face. Wilma stared up at it and was puzzled by how so much noise could come from something so tiny.

She took the poster and ran back towards the Academy. Slipping through the front door, she closed it behind her, shoving the stone nose back to its original position. The Academy sanatorium was on the ground floor and Wilma skipped down the corridor with its polished tiles adorned with magnifying glasses and word puzzles. Mr Goodman always told Wilma that the biggest part of being a detective was the ability to work tricky things out. And the puzzles that adorned the Academy were there for practice. Not that Wilma had had much time to solve them, of course, because in the eight weeks since starting at the Academy she'd already helped Mr Goodman on two cases.

Kite was sitting on the sanatorium examination table, smearing herself with a thick green ointment. 'It takes away the sting,' she explained. 'It's quite good. Although it does smell like the inside of a cat's ear.'

'Here's the poster, Miss Lambard,' said Wilma, handing it over. 'The man said we have to display it and attend all three ceremonies.'

'Yes.' Kite nodded. 'It's the same every ten years. Do you know how the Cooper government works?'

Wilma shook her head.

'Well,' said Kite, clearing her throat, 'Cooper Island is a

19

tombolocracy. And that means that every ten years the Grand Tombola is brought out and paraded through the streets and set on the Ceremonial Platform. That's the first ceremony, the Ceremonial Parade. Then at the second ceremony, the Placing of the Names, all the names of everyone eligible for the election are placed into the Grand Tombola. Then on the third day, at the Final Naming Ceremony, the present Cooperate General, that's Glenda Blaize, draws a name from the tombola and whoever's name it is becomes the new Cooperate General for the next ten years. They take charge straight away. And they're allowed to pass three new laws on the spot.'

'I see. What happens if it's someone who doesn't want to be the Cooperate General?' asked Wilma.

'That hasn't happened yet. Although once a five-year-old's name got into the tombola by accident and her name was drawn. She was called Ffyona Jennyson. The first law she passed was that everything should be made of toffee. It was chaos. Nothing could be done about it, of course. Once a name is picked, that's it.'

'So I could be a Cooperate General?' said Wilma excitedly.

'No,' explained Kite. 'Only Farsider names over the age of twenty-one and a half – usually – go into the tombola. And you're from the Lowside.'

Cooper Island, situated somewhere between England and

France, was an odd little place. A combination of laziness and indifference meant the outside world had never bothered to discover it and so Cooper chugged along with its own strange ways and peculiar habits, untroubled by anything that might be happening beyond its shores. Divided long ago by a great wall with a gate in it, the Farside, where Wilma now lived, was the well-to-do bit, whereas the Lowside, where Wilma had come from, was regarded as the slightly stinky relative. A bit like a distant cousin with bad teeth and dubious personal hygiene who comes for Christmas and burps all through lunch. A bit like that. It was quite wrong that this was the way it was, of course, but old habits die hard. It was simply the way things were.

Wilma frowned. 'It doesn't seem fair that Lowsiders aren't allowed to enter the draw. Although it is understandable. The Lowside is chock-a-block with Criminal Elements. But not every Lowsider is a wrong'un. I'm not. And neither is Mr Goodman and he came from the Lowside. Actually, now I think about it, I know LOADS of Lowsiders who are really nice and good. It's a shame we're a bit tinted with a wrong brush.'

'Ah. Here you both are,' sounded a voice behind them.

Let's get one thing clear from the off. Theodore P. Goodman, Cooper's most famous and serious detective was a very impressive man. Tall, handsome, brave and brilliant at throwing balls overarm, there was very little he couldn't do. As he stood

21

before them, his deep green overcoat flapping behind him, Wilma looked up and grinned. She LOVED being his apprentice.

'Hello, Mr Goodman,' she said, beaming. 'Today I bugged a room and was chased by snakes. And I've been spying and spooking. And Pickle was a chicken.'

'Chicken? Spooking? Snaking?' asked Inspector Lemone, who had come in behind Theodore and was dabbing his sweating forehead with a handkerchief. Lemone's eyes narrowed slightly. No. He'd ask no further questions. It was probably for the best. He'd just eat a corn crumble biscuit instead.

All great detectives, as anyone knows, need a loyal, if slightly slow, assistant and Inspector Lemone was just that. It's fair to say that he knew nothing at all about crime fighting and had only become a policeman due to an unfortunate clerical error in the Cooper Employment Office. There are two facts you need to know about Inspector Lemone: his love of biscuits and his secret love of Mrs Speckle, Theodore's woollen-clad housekeeper. That's it. So let's move on.

'I have come to fetch you, Wilma,' continued Theodore, his moustache twitching a little. 'We're off to the office of Glenda Blaize.'

Wilma's eyes widened. 'The Cooperate General?' she asked, excited. 'But she's famous! Why does she want to see us?'

'She sent me a message that she has some important

information,' said Lemone, chewing his biscuit and reaching for his notebook. He flicked it open and, mouth still full, read, '*Information that may shatter the very foundations of every belief system this island has ever had.* That's what she said.'

Everyone stared at him. He swallowed. 'She's probably exaggerating,' he added.

Let's hope she is, eh, readers?

23

Chapter 3

As Wilma and Pickle bounced along in the trailer attached to the back of Theodore and Lemone's tandem, the young apprentice marvelled at how her life had turned out. Only two months ago, she had been stuck at the Institute for Woeful Children with nothing to look forward to and with little to no idea of where she had come from. And now here she was, taken on as Theodore P. Goodman's apprentice, with proper leads to her own mystery and whizzing off to another exciting case. It was incredible. Not only that, but as she looked down at the beagle at her feet she marvelled at how he was the best friend and assistant an apprentice detective could ever ask for. How glad she was that she and Pickle had found each other so soon after she'd left the Institute and how lonely she'd have been without him, before finding Mr Goodman. She loved him dearly.

The office of Glenda Blaize was at the very top of the

Cooper parliament building, a grand old structure that stood at the north end of the Avenue of the Cooperans. The view of Cooper from her windows was breathtaking and Wilma stood, hands and nose pressed up against the pane, looking out over the Central Plaza, filled with sugarcane swizzle trees, to the one small hill on the horizon. She'd never been this high up before. It was quite something.

Glenda, the presiding Cooperate General, was behind Wilma, sitting astride the stuffed Donkey of Office having her portrait finished before she gave up her term in charge. Beside her hunched a thin, weedy-looking man. He had a pale complexion and wore small, round glasses. Wilma stared at him. He sort of looked like an uncooked chicken. Next to him was a scholarly-looking woman holding lots of official documents. In front of them, next to the painter who was applying final touches to the portrait, was Captain Brock, head of the 2nd Hawks Brigade. Trained to look in four directions at once, he could locate anything in his peripheral vision in under three seconds. It was quite a skill.

The 2nd Hawks Brigade was made up of Cooper's finest servicemen. Apart from Theodore and Inspector Lemone, they were the island's only law enforcement, and on important days like this it fell to Captain Brock to devise all manner of strategic hoo-ha. Hoo-ha, in case you don't know, is the proper name given to those bits in meetings where adults glaze over and stop paying attention. You know. Or like when teachers try to explain the intricacies of long division. It's a bit like that.

Captain Brock was standing next to a blackboard with a map of Central Coop chalked on to it and was in the midst of giving an official briefing of the running order for the first ceremony, the Ceremonial Parade.

'So at the end of the parade,' he was explaining, pointing towards the blackboard with his swagger-stick, 'you will escort the Grand Tombola to the platform and, once in place, you will draw the curtains so that it remains encircled until the Placing of the Names.'

'There's an Official Green Completion Form that needs to be filled in after that happens,' said the scholarly-looking woman, whose name was Melba Toest. She was the Keeper of Cooper Law and held the National Record for the Most Library Cards Alphabetized in an Hour.

'It's the twenty-fifth paper down in the second pile on the desk,' said Captain Brock, quick as a flash.

'Oh! So it is. Thank you.'

'Do you think *I* should draw the curtains round the tombola?' chipped in the weedy-looking man, shoving his glasses up his nose. 'Might make things easier.'

'No thank you, Dromley,' said Glenda, trying to maintain her pose. 'The responsibility for drawing the curtains rests with the Cooperate General, not the Cooperate's secretary.'

'But you might be busy, waving at the people and so forth. You could make a speech and then gesture towards me—'

'Dromley,' interrupted Glenda, 'you're being whiny again. Do stop.'

The secretary screwed his lips into a tight ball.

'And that's it!' declared the artist, a red-haired woman in a paint-spattered beret and a pale blue smock. 'I'm done. You can get down now and have a look if you like.'

Glenda heaved a sigh of relief and relaxed her pose. 'Thank goodness,' she said, hopping down from the Donkey of Office. 'I've been up here for three days.' As she dismounted, everyone followed her to gather around the portrait. The artist was wiping her paintbrushes and looked mighty pleased.

'What do you think?' she asked, gesturing towards the finished painting.

Glenda stared, her mouth dropping open. Wilma couldn't believe her eyes. It was, quite possibly, the worst painting she'd ever seen.

'Pickle could have done better than—' she began, before being nudged sharply by Mr Goodman.

'It's . . . interesting,' said Glenda eventually.

'Is the eye supposed to be down there?' asked Lemone, pointing. 'The face looks like it's melted.'

The artist glared at them. 'Philistines!' she cried, before storming from the room.

'Three days on a stuffed donkey,' said Glenda, shaking her head. 'Anyway, Mr Goodman, thank you for coming. Have you met Dromley Abbams, my secretary?' she added, gesturing to her aide.

'No. I don't believe I have,' said the great detective, extending his hand.

Dromley shook it limply.

'Then let's get down to business,' said Glenda, striding towards her desk. She flicked open a small mahogany box filled with cigars, pulled one out, bit the end off and lit it with a lighter shaped like a lion's head. Turning, she put one leg up on a chair and stuck her thumbs into the corners of her waistcoat. 'I am in receipt of some startling information!' she declared, taking a deep puff of her cigar.

Everyone stared at her.

'Some startling information that, if true,' she continued, 'could destroy the very fabric of Cooper society!'

Wilma's eyes widened and she shot a look across the room towards Inspector Lemone. He was trying to eat another corn crumble biscuit, but very, very quietly, while Pickle was staring

up at him hoping he'd drop a crumb. No chance. The inspector caught Wilma's eye and raised his eyebrows. It was exactly as he'd said! How exciting!

'Dromley,' Glenda barked, 'tell them what you told me!'

The secretary cleared his throat. 'The thing is,' he began, 'I take my job very seriously. Who knows what horrors lurk beyond the Great Wall. Criminal Elements are notoriously untrustworthy so if I'd let someone else deliver the election posters who knows where they'd have ended up and we certainly wouldn't know what we know now. Which is some very important information.'

He stopped, as if expecting a word of praise.

Inspector Lemone gave out a light cough. 'Sorry,' he said, as everyone glanced in his direction. 'Crumb went down the wrong way.'

Pickle, still staring, drooled.

Dromley, looking a little disappointed, ploughed on. 'Someone else might have ignored it. Someone else might not have understood the matter's gravity, the seriousness of its implications. Someone else might have done nothing about it. Someone else—'

'Oh, do stop building your part up, Dromley,' barked Glenda. 'Spit it out!'

Dromley shot his boss a short, resentful look. 'The long and the short of it, Mr Goodman,' he continued, stepping closer to the detective, 'is that I went to the Lowside first thing this morning to distribute election posters. As we all know, Lowsiders are not entitled to be named in the Placing of the Names Ceremony, but they are required to attend. And it was when I was sticking up a poster in the Twelve Rats' Tails that I overheard something quite interesting.' He paused for effect. 'Something very interesting indeed.'

'Well, what was it?' asked Theodore, his jaw setting tight.

'A dastardly deed is to take place during the Ten-Annual Election,' whispered Dromley, leaning even closer.

Wilma frowned. 'But what dastardly deed? And which ceremony? There are three.'

'That, I cannot tell you,' said Dromley. 'I am merely the messenger. A witness to several Criminal Elements huddled together discussing some tittle-tattle about a terrible crime to be committed right here, on the Farside of Cooper, in the next three days.'

Theodore's moustache twitched. 'This is all terribly vague, Mr Abbams,' he said, twiddling the magnifying glass that hung from his waistcoat pocket. 'Do you have nothing specific? Criminal Elements are constantly hatching plots at the Twelve Rats' Tails. Are you sure it wasn't a case of drunken boasting?'

Dromley shrugged his shoulders. 'I can only tell you what I

overheard. I am not the famous detective – you are. You may do with the information as you wish.'

'The thing is,' interrupted Glenda, flicking her cigar ash into an upturned crocodile-jaw ashtray, 'that if it is true then what could the dastardly deed be? And I've given this some thought. Why commit a crime during the Ten-Annual Ceremonies? It must be an attempt to scupper the election. And for that reason, Mr Goodman, I would like you to investigate this matter to the full.'

Theodore thought seriously for a moment and nodded. 'I think you're right, Madam Cooperate. The election is the most important date in a decade. The future of Cooper depends upon it. If Mr Abbams's claims are substantiated, then I'm afraid we have a very serious matter on our hands. Possibly the most serious case of my career.'

Wilma nodded. 'And we've got absolutely nothing to go on,' she said, trying to be helpful. 'Nothing at all.'

'Not quite nothing, Wilma,' answered Theodore, thinking on his feet. 'We have the Twelve Rats' Tails. That will be our starting point.'

'And you do know who's staying there at the moment, don't you?' chipped in Lemone, flushing a little at the thought. 'Barbu D'Anvers. The rottenest scoundrel on the island. He's taken rooms. He'll be behind this, I'll wager.'

Wilma twisted the bottom of her pinafore in her hands.

31

Hearing Barbu's name again was something of a shock. Not only had she recently learned that she might be connected to Max and Pru, but she'd also discovered that Theodore's long-time nemesis and the man who was constantly threatening to kill her had been the one who had delivered her as a baby to the innkeeper at the Twelve Rats' Tails. It was the innkeeper who had taken her to the Institute for Woeful Children, but why had Barbu been the one to hand her over? Was Barbu D'Anvers Wilma's father? She certainly hoped not.

'Yes,' agreed Theodore, with some resolve, 'I think it's time we kept a closer eye on Mr D'Anvers. Ever since he was declared bankrupt, I'm sure he's been constantly plotting, trying to find a way to get rich again and buy back his home, Rascal Rock. And he'd love nothing more than to get back at the authorities who seized his assets.' Theodore took a deep breath then turned to face Glenda. 'Thank you, Madam Cooperate. We shall commence our investigations immediately. Captain Brock, I think in the circumstances you and your men should keep a twenty-four-hour guard over Miss Blaize until we know more. There isn't a moment to lose. Lemone! Wilma! Let's head back to Clarissa Cottage and formulate a plan!'

A dastardly deed afoot? But *who's* behind it? And *what* is it? On to the next page, quick! Let's get this case rolling!

Chapter 4

Barbu D'Anvers had had just about enough. He was sitting with his head slumped into the palm of his hand, and wearing a scowl like thunder. Tiny in stature, he was wearing a shabby brown jacket that was far too big for him. He looked like a stick in a sack. Next to him, dressed in matching brown jackets, were his evil apprentice, Janty, a young boy with a shock of black curly hair, who was juggling three daggers in the air, and his thuggish henchman, Tully, who was standing, eyes closed, singing one of Cooper's traditional folk songs.

'I was in old Coop town, a-hoo diddly-oh!
And there was a lady, all bells and all bow,
But she had a face that looked like a crow!
And a massive big belly that wobbled like dough!
With a diddle diddle diddle diddle diddle de-doe!

And a piddle piddle piddle piddle piddle pie-po!
And a tiddle tiddle tiddle tiddle tiddle ty-toe!
And a riddle riddle riddle riddle riddle ry-roe!
Let's all go for a pie!'

Barbu D'Anvers was, as anyone knows, Cooper Island's most wicked villain. As fellows go, he was the very worst. He kicked kittens, poked old ladies in the eye and NEVER shared his tangerines. He had, up until a few months ago, been the master of all he surveyed, but, due to a bureaucratic technicality at the conclusion of the Case of the Putrid Poison, he had been tossed from his home at Rascal Rock and had all his property seized. He was penniless. And it was making him FURIOUS.

Barbu looked out at the audience of Criminal Elements all singing along and waving their tankards in the air. Had it come to this? Barbu D'Anvers, the greatest Criminal Element Cooper Island had ever seen, sitting on a shabby stage, wearing a brown entertainer's jacket that smelt of sour milk, doing turns for petty thieves? He heaved a sigh.

'You're on, master,' whispered Janty, giving him a nudge as Tully's song came to an end.

Barbu curled his top lip and pushed himself up from his chair. As he walked towards the centre of the stage, Tully was still taking his bow, the audience on their feet, drunkenly baying for more songs.

'Get off –' Barbu gestured towards his henchman – 'and let me get this over with.'

A smattering of boos broke out among the audience.

'Shut up,' snapped Barbu. 'And now for some magic,' he continued, scowling. 'You there,' he added, pointing towards a man in a flat cap smoking a long clay pipe. 'Come here.'

The man pointed towards himself, his eyebrows raised. Another great cheer went up from the audience.

Barbu rolled his eyes. 'Come on! Come on! I haven't got all day!'

The man, encouraged by his friends, came up on to the stage and stood, grinning inanely.

Barbu held out a hand. 'Give me your pocket purse,' he said irritably. 'I'm going to make it disappear.'

A huge 'OOOOOOOOH' went up from the crowd. Laughing, the man reached into his coat pocket and pulled out a weighty leather pouch filled with groggles. Barbu snatched it. Placing a handkerchief over his clenched fist, the villain half-heartedly waved the fingers of his other hand, said 'Shazam!' in a sarcastic tone and then pulled the handkerchief off with a flourish. The pouch was gone.

'OOOOOOOOOH,' went the crowd again. The man whose

35

pouch it was stared in amazement until Barbu started to shoo him off the stage.

The man blinked. 'But where's my pocket purse?'

Barbu looked at him as if he was stupid. 'I said I'd make it disappear,' he scowled. 'Not come BACK again! Tully, toss him from the stage. That's it. End of show! We're done.'

Pushing past a group of baying patrons, Barbu ducked through a back door and threw his brown jacket to the ground. Tully and Janty were hard on his heels.

'How many *more* have we got to do today?' yelled Barbu, slumping into a tatty armchair.

'Sixteen,' said Tully, consulting a poster of show times on the back of the door.

'SIXTEEN! This is slave labour,' wailed Barbu. 'I'm not even a member of a reputable entertainers' union! Why aren't people up in arms? I've had NO TRAINING!'

'At least you managed to get some more money, master,' said Janty, pulling out the pocket purse he'd been secretly thrown during the onstage trick. 'If we can do that sixteen more times today, then our takings will be quite decent. We'll be back living at Rascal Rock in no time!'

'DECENT?' screamed the diminutive rogue, his face turning purple. 'Since when does Barbu D'Anvers aspire to a wage that's DECENT? I want riches supreme! I want to live in a house made from crushed swans and eat animals that are near extinct! I want excess! I want fine wines! I don't want to be sitting in the back of a filthy inn wearing a coat made from unnatural fibres while inebriated men jeer at me!' Barbu picked up a half-filled tankard that was sitting on a table next to him and threw it against the wall with a mighty yell. Running a hand through his voluminous hair, he stuck out his chin. 'Right. I feel better now I've broken something. Is there any chance of me being allowed to kill someone later?'

'Not really, no,' frowned Janty, with a shake of his head.

Tully took out a crumpled piece of paper from his inside coat pocket and looked at it. 'It's because we're on the bed and cabaret package, Mr Barbu. We could upgrade to the Deluxe Evil package. That comes with killing AND extortion.'

'How much is that one?' Barbu sniffed.

'Five groggles per person, per night.'

'FIVE groggles? It's almost as if they don't WANT anyone to commit a murder. What is this place coming to? I remember when the Lowside was a stinking cesspit of evil. Now look at it. It's all folksongs and laughing! And having fun!'

'Maybe that'll change come the Ten-Annual Election,' suggested Janty. 'I saw someone putting the posters up for it earlier. Perhaps the new Cooperate General will make everything dreadful.'

'Not much chance of that,' replied Barbu huffily. 'Now put a Lowsider in charge and we might see some PROPER changes.'

'Lowsiders aren't allowed to be in the election,' said Tully, sticking a small sausage in his ear to scratch it.

'Yes!' barked Barbu. 'I KNOW THAT. More's the pity. How long till we have to do our next show?'

Janty walked over to the back of the door to check the schedule. 'Ten minutes,' he replied and then, staring up at another poster that was pinned next to it, added, 'Have you seen this, master? It's a poster for a Villains' Ball.'

'Villains' Ball?' Barbu's eyes narrowed. 'Who's organizing that? Pull the poster down – bring it to me.'

'Who's he?' asked Barbu, as he took the notice and pointed to the picture of a masked man at the top of it. Tully and Janty shrugged. 'What's this? *Inviting all Criminal Elements to attend a spectacular Villains' Ball*. Hang on . . . there's small print. *Tickets may include a dastardly plan to destroy the Farside as we know it*.' Barbu frowned. 'Interesting. Either of you know anything about this?'

Tully and Janty shook their heads.

Suddenly from outside the room there was a huge commotion. Barbu pushed past Janty to open the door and look through into the inn. Standing on the raised stage was a moustachioed man in tight-fitting breeches. He had long thigh-length boots on, a frilled shirt and a black tapered frock coat. He was also wearing a mask.

'It's him,' whispered Barbu, gesturing to the others to come and look.

In the bar, the drinkers were cheering. The masked man raised a hand for quiet. 'The time of the Lowsider has arrived!' he cried in a slightly shrill voice. 'Come to my Villains' Ball and I shall reveal a dastardly plan to bring the Farside to its knees!' And, with that, he threw down a smoke bomb and disappeared. The room was in uproar.

Barbu D'Anvers closed the door slowly and stood in thought. 'OK. He's sort of stealing my act. But even I, the greatest rogue that ever walked this island, am forced to confess that he *was* impressive. Thrilling even. And he did have lovely boots. Did you see them, Janty? I think they had a heel.'

Janty and Tully exchanged a quick look.

But Barbu was oblivious, his eyes suddenly aflame. 'I'm sick of scrabbling for scraps. My fiendishness needs to flourish. It's time to get out of the mess we find ourselves in. We must meet this fellow at the first opportunity! I need an idea. And it has to be HORRIBLE! Everyone who has crossed me is going to PAY! Be warned, Cooper! I'm on a rampage of REVENGE!'

Watch out, everyone. Barbu is back.

Chapter 5

It was one of Wilma's jobs, as apprentice to Cooper's most famous and serious detective, to make a Clue Board whenever they had a new case. A Clue Board is a vital tool in the detective's cupboard. It's a visual catch-up of everything discovered to date, like a desk-tidy for facts and hunches. At the start of any new investigation, detectives are usually presented with a crime and a bag of clues that require deciphering, but, in this instance, Theodore and Wilma were facing a blank page. No crime had yet been committed and, to be honest, it had Wilma in a muddle. Because they didn't really have anything to go on, Wilma had had to be extra creative and so she'd covered the Clue Board with a hand-drawn map of Cooper and then pinned various things on to it to show all the places that might be targets for the Dastardly Deed that was about to be committed.

'I have called it,' declared Wilma, pointing towards the Clue

Board she had assembled on Mr Goodman's desk in the cosy living room of his, Wilma and Pickle's home, Clarissa Cottage, 'the Case of the Robbing or Murders or Kidnaps or other Unpleasantness to do with the Unknown Thing or Things. I think that covers everything.'

She'd used a small cotton cow to represent the Grand Groggle Depository, a blue glove for the National Museum of Cooper and several slimy pieces of half-shredded rope for every bank on the island. A slightly chewed toffee represented the Cooper parliament building while several dirty paw prints signified the homes of the wealthier citizens of the Farside. To finish off, a scattering of smiley faces acted as markers for every shop and tavern. In short, the Clue Board was smothered.

Inspector Lemone took a closer look. 'What's that?' he asked, pointing to a half-eaten pear core nailed over one corner of the island.

'The Pearl Emporium, of course,' said Wilma, with a firm nod.

Inspector Lemone looked baffled.

'You know,' explained Wilma. 'Pear. Pearl. It's almost the same word . . . Oh never mind.'

'So what you have done, Wilma,' said Theodore, patting her on the back reassuringly, 'is to concentrate on all the locations on the island with financial value. And why have you done that?'

Wilma blinked. This was one of those situations called 'being put on the spot'. She'd read about this in her Academy handbook in the chapter entitled 'Ideas and How to Have Them'.

'Well,' she began, clearing her throat, 'you know how you always tell me to try to think about things in a wonky way? Well, I started thinking about what sort of dastardly deeds the Criminal Elements on the Lowside get up to. And, although it is the Ten-Annual Election and everything, there's one thing the Criminal Elements are always after. And that's groggles. And then I thought, if the Criminal Elements want groggles, then where would they get them? So that's when I came up with the idea of identifying every place on the Farside that has loads of groggles or precious things in it.'

42

'You may be right, Wilma. I've never known a Criminal Element who didn't want more groggles.'

Wilma beamed. So far, so good. And she hadn't broken anything yet. This case was getting off to the best start imaginable.

'But if you are right,' continued Theodore, 'then we have a very obvious problem. You have listed multiple targets. How do we pick which of them is most at risk? We can't cover all of them, all of the time, for three whole days. Especially when we'll be so busy with the ceremonies as well – which I'm sure is the point!'

Wilma chewed her bottom lip. 'I don't know, Mr Goodman,' she began. 'I could put all the place names in my pinafore pocket and pick one out?'

'Far from ideal,' said the detective, taking a puff on his favourite pipe. 'We are facing a situation in which we may be seeking to protect one or multiple unknown targets. We have no idea who is planning what and, with three ceremonies approaching, we are completely in the dark as to which day the Criminal Elements will strike. At best, we have three days to solve this case. At worst, we have only one.'

Wilma nodded and tried walking up and down with her hands behind her back the way she had seen her mentor do when he was thinking deeply.

'Perhaps,' she suggested, holding a finger in the air, 'the ceremonies are the bunch of keys to things?'

'Just one key, Wilma,' explained Theodore, with a small twitch of his moustache. 'When you are looking for answers, you only need one key to something.'

'Well, that's something to feel positive about!' said Wilma, raising her arms. 'Only *one* key! Which, you know, narrows things down.'

'Hmm . . . anyway, you're right. It's no coincidence that something is being hatched at the same time as the Ten-Annual Ceremonies. It might be useful for us to think about what happens at each one.'

Wilma blinked about ten times. She'd been right TWICE in the space of five minutes. This was her best day as an apprentice EVER.

'I can do that!' chipped in Inspector Lemone, helping himself to the plate of corn crumbles that Mrs Speckle, Theodore's housekeeper, had brought in moments before. 'I love the Ten-Annual Ceremonies. At the first one, when the tombola is paraded through town, you get the wet cakes. Then in the second one, when the names are placed in the tombola, you get hot jacks, popped jamblies and candy flan, and then in the last ceremony, which takes for ever and ever, and includes the actual name pulling, you get the twenty-five-course snack plate. I love that.'

'That's it!' said Theodore, clicking his fingers together. 'Blow me down, Lemone, but you've actually said something sensible. The last ceremony does go on for a considerable length of time. Over five hours, in fact. And, if we think logically, then what does that tell us, Wilma?'

'That we need to take sandwiches?' she asked eagerly.

'No, that it allows more time for dastardly deeds to unfold. I may be wrong, but I suspect whatever is going to happen will take place during the Final Naming Ceremony!'

'Good idea about the sandwiches though,' added Inspector Lemone, giving Wilma a nudge.

Pickle nodded. There could never be enough sandwiches.

'We need to sharpen our wits and steel our resolve. Every moment is going to count. Wilma's Clue Board has made one thing sparklingly clear – we know absolutely nothing. So, as I suspected, we need to start at the source. Lemone, Wilma, up sticks. We're going to the Twelve Rats' Tails!'

Generally speaking, when your only hope is a putrid den of unpleasantness tinged with a musk of overwhelming body odour, it's time for everyone to worry.

So start worrying.

Chapter 6

'**O**h, hello,' said Trevor, the Great Gate border guard, staring suspiciously down in the direction of the apprentice detective. 'It's you again.'

Trevor, the rotund, over-uniformed border official who oversaw every crossing between the Farside and the Lowside of Cooper Island had what we like to call 'form' with Wilma. He liked his border crossings to be as bureaucratic and ship-shape as possible, something that Wilma had no interest in whatsoever.

'Papers,' Trevor said, eyeing his small nemesis and her beagle.

Wilma stuck her thumb behind her silver apprentice-detective badge and shoved it upward. 'I don't need papers any more, Trevor,' she began. 'Don't you remember? I'm Mr Goodman's apprentice detective. You gave me an Impertinence Order once. Well, not you, but the Official Border Peepers did.' Wilma turned and waved towards the four sets of eyes that were staring out at her from a slit in the wall next to Trevor's booth. Trevor's eyes widened in mild panic.

'No waving at the peepers, if you please,' he spluttered. 'They find it most upsetting. As well you know.' He peered down at Wilma's badge.

Wilma cast her eyes sideways. In the bottom right-hand corner of Trevor's booth window there was a small purple poster. She frowned.

'Mr Goodman,' she called towards the parked tandem behind her. 'I think you might like to see this.'

Dismounting, the great and serious detective strode over towards the border booth. He gave a short, polite nod to Trevor. 'Everything in order?' he asked. 'We are quite pressed for time.'

Trevor, who was always slightly flustered in the presence of people with proper authority, stood up to salute, but as he did so he dropped his heap of crossing files, sending paper scattering all over the ground.

'Mr Goodman . . .' he began, trying to salute and pick up papers simultaneously. 'I'll just stamp you in . . . I mean . . . I . . .'

Wilma tugged at Mr Goodman's sleeve. 'Look at this poster,' she said, as Trevor scrabbled about on the ground. 'Do you think it's important?'

47

'*Inviting all Criminal Elements to attend a spectacular Villains' Ball . . .*' the great detective read out, slowly and thoughtfully.

'Look at the smaller bit down there,' said Wilma, pointing to the bottom of the poster.

'*Tickets may include a dastardly plan to destroy the Farside as we know it*. Hmmm. And look at the date, Wilma. It's tonight!'

'It's a lovely colour, isn't it, Mr Goodman?'

'It's happening immediately after the Ceremonial Parade. That can't be a coincidence. And you're right, Wilma, but it's not just lovely, it's a very unusual colour. Trevor . . .' he added, 'who gave you this poster to put up?'

Trevor was still on his hands and knees. A wooden hand had shot out from the hole in the peepers' wall and was poking at him with some insistence.

'Yes, all right!' he yelled. 'Just hang on!' He stood up, flustered, and shoved his hat back to its rightful angle. 'Strictly speaking, Mr Goodman, I'm not really allowed to tell anyone anything about the border booth. Very secret. Very hush-hush. Very, very official.'

Theodore stretched his shoulders back and stared intently at Trevor, twitching his magnificent moustache.

Trevor gulped. 'But, seeing as it's you, Mr Goodman, I suppose I can tell you. The answer is – I'm not really sure. Didn't see the fellow's face. He was wearing a mask.'

'Would you let me take the poster? It may be an important piece of evidence.'

'It says it's just for Criminal Elements,' noted Wilma, as Trevor removed the poster from its holder. 'And, look, there's a Masked Man on it. Who do you think that is? I wonder what happens at a Villains' Ball . . . Do you think they all sit around coming up with dastardly plans? Crumbs, Mr Goodman, this poster is as gigantic a clue as they come. What are we going to do?'

'Excellent questions, Wilma. I think we shall have to attend this Villains' Ball,' answered Theodore, reaching for his magnifying glass as he took the poster from Trevor. 'And find ourselves some answers.'

'But how will we get in?' asked Wilma, trying to peer over Theodore's arm to get a closer look. 'Everyone knows we're not Criminal Elements.'

'Remember your top tips, Wilma? Which one might help us in this situation?'

'Top tip number seven, Mr Goodman!' Wilma grinned. 'Using a disguise can sometimes be cunning! And, not only that, but we can add in some espionage as well. It'll be like double cunning.'

'This ink is *very* unusual,' mumbled Theodore, peering through his magnifying glass. He handed the poster to Wilma.

'We're going to need to get this to Penbert for analysis and then we're going to need disguises. We'll head over to the lab after we've been to the Twelve Rats' Tails and then I'll send you to sort out the outfits. I wouldn't normally place so much responsibility on your shoulders, Wilma, but we're up against it. Think you can manage?'

Wilma nodded enthusiastically. This race against time meant she got to do loads more than normal. It was brilliant.

Rotten-Egg Alley, the filth-strewn lane that led to the Twelve Rats' Tails, was, as ever, seeping with malicious intent. Criminal Elements huddled in shadows, ready for all manner of dodgy dealings. As Theodore and his team made their way towards the tatty inn door, Wilma caught the eye of a man with a wooden leg. His teeth were blackened, his face torn with scars. He opened his great overcoat to reveal a treasure trove of trinkets.

'Something pretty for the little lady?' he whispered.

Wilma shook her head vehemently and walked on, Pickle hard on her heels and growling defensively.

'Stay close to Inspector Lemone, Wilma,' advised Theodore as his hand rested on the faded brass serpent that slithered down the front panel of the entrance.

There was quite the commotion as they entered the tavern. People were on their feet, tankards aloft, singing rowdily, so that Theodore and the team were able to creep their way in relatively unnoticed.

'They're certainly enjoying their squifty juice,' muttered Lemone, giving his sweaty forehead a wipe in the stuffy air.

To their surprise, ahead of them on the staged area, was Barbu grimacing as Tully led the customers in a rousing version of 'Lowside La-de-dah', a favourite tune that served as an unofficial anthem for the island's Criminal Elements. Wilma peeked out from behind Theodore and caught Janty's eye. He frowned as he saw her and who she was with and leaned over to whisper into his master's ear. Barbu's head spun in their direction. He raised a hand for quiet but, being ignored, he picked up a stool and cracked it round the back of Tully's head.

'BE QUIET!' he yelled, tossing the broken stool leg to the floor as Tully rubbed his head. 'We have company and it isn't someone bearing glad tidings. Watch yourself, everyone. Theodore P. Goodman has entered the building.'

A great gasp went out and the sound of chairs scraping the floor filled the room as people turned to stare at the great detective. Wilma gulped. The air was thick with tension and hostility. Pickle let out a small warning growl.

'Now what would you want here, Goodman?' Barbu sneered. 'Seen the error of your ways? Decided to come back to the people you've betrayed? We all know you're Lowsider-

51

born. And yet you have dedicated your life to putting us behind bars.'

A low discontented grumble sounded through the tavern parlour.

Theodore's jaw set tight. 'Lowsiders have never been forced to turn to crime, Barbu. We may have been dealt hard cards in life, but wrongdoing isn't the answer. I am a proud Lowsider, through and through. But I learned long ago that you will never change people's minds through force. Lead by example and good deeds. Use your mind, not your fists. Only then will we earn the respect we so long for.'

Barbu curled his lip. 'Ugh. You're so EARNEST. I didn't ask for a lecture. Anyway, what do you want?'

Theodore pushed his way through the throng to the front of the stage. 'Perhaps it would be better,' he began, fixing his nemesis with a firm stare, 'if we had a word in private.'

'All right,' snapped Barbu scornfully, 'Back room. Now.' The rascal looked back out at the audience. 'Show's over, thank goodness. Go away.'

A cacophony of boos rang out as Barbu, flanked by Tully and Janty, left the stage with Theodore, Wilma, Pickle and Inspector Lemone in tow.

The dressing room behind the stage was a tiny, dingy affair, no bigger than a broom cupboard. It was full of old dusty furniture and a smell of damp hung in the air. There was no window, so the only light came from a dim gas lamp.

Inspector Lemone, who was bringing up the rear, peered over Theodore's shoulder as he tried to get through the door. 'Quite a squeeze in here. Could you . . . if Wilma moves to the left . . . I can . . .'

'Don't put your elbow in my eye, Tully,' barked Barbu, as the burly henchman tried to squash himself into a space by an upturned table.

'Sorry,' said Lemone, his face flattened against a mirror on the wall. 'If I can just hook my leg over there and . . .'

'I can hold Pickle,' called out Wilma, from the middle of the scrum. 'That'll give us more room!'

'Small ones at the front!' yelled Tully, leaning against the table and breaking it. 'Ow!' he added, as Barbu rapped him on the forehead sharply with his cane.

'I am not SMALL,' he bellowed, as he was pressed forward in the crush. 'I am the most IMPORTANT. THAT is why I am at the front. Do you understand?'

'Yes, Mr Barbu,' answered Tully, wincing. Again.

'Right then,' said Barbu, turning and finding himself nose to nose with Pickle. 'No. Don't lick me. I think the quicker we get this over with the better.'

'Do you know anything about a crime intended to take place

during the Ten-Annual Ceremonies?' said Theodore, towering over the diminutive rogue.

'No,' said Barbu, lying. 'No idea what you're talking about. And, even if I did, the fact you think I'd tell you is hilarious. Tully! Janty! Laugh in their faces!'

'I can't, master,' wheezed the boy, crushed up against a coat stand. 'Quite hard to . . . breathe.'

'And what about this?' continued Theodore, shoving the poster into Barbu's face. 'Have you got anything to do with it?'

Wilma, who hadn't blinked since finding herself so close to Barbu, could feel her heart thumping against her chest. This might be her only chance to get to the bottom of her own mystery. Barbu had been the one to leave her with the tavern's innkeeper. She had to know how and why!

'You left me here ten years ago . . .' she began breathlessly.

'Sorry?' interrupted Barbu immediately. 'Did anyone express any interest in you? No. They did not. You should take a leaf out of *my* apprentice's book. He doesn't speak unless I let him.'

Wilma shot a look in Janty's direction where he was squashed up next to her. 'I don't know why you still work for him,' she muttered, hoisting Pickle a little higher in her arms. 'He's SO horrible. And he beat up your father. In the Case of the Frozen Hearts. I've got the newspaper report on my Clue Ring.'

Barbu blew a small raspberry. 'It's my JOB to rough over people. That's what being evil IS. And, besides, I didn't KILL him. That was that other fellow. The one with the poisoned dart.'

Wilma held Janty's gaze, but the boy said nothing and cast his eyes downward instead.

'Answer my question, D'Anvers,' insisted Theodore, his eyes narrowing. 'Are you behind this ball?'

Barbu shook his head a little and assumed an expression of mock bafflement. 'I don't know why you're asking me. Masks don't suit me. OH! OH, WHAT IS THAT SMELL?'

A terrible heavy, rancid stink had filled the room. Wilma threw her head backwards, her tongue lolling out in disgust.

'Oh, Pickle! NOT NOW!'

The beagle tried to muster a small, sheepish look of regret. But it was no good. He *loved* the smell of his own farts.

'Everyone out!' cried Lemone, scrabbling to open the door. 'Fresh air! We must have fresh air!'

As they all bundled back out into the tavern, coughing and spluttering, Theodore, standing tall, turned to face his nemesis once more. 'I shall be keeping a very close eye on you, D'Anvers. One false move and you won't see the light of day again.'

Tully reached up and opened a window for some air. 'I don't know why you're bothering Mr D'Anvers,' he muttered. 'It's

55

the Masked Man you want to find. He's the one who's organized the Villains' Ball. He was in here yesterday.'

Barbu shot his stupid henchman a look of utter disdain. 'Tully! Shut up!'

'Oh,' said the thick sidekick, raising a hand to his mouth. 'Did I say that out loud? Although . . . isn't that in the Evil Code? *Always* put the blame on someone else?'

'A Masked Man was here?' pressed Theodore, turning to look back at Barbu. 'And what did he say? Did you speak to him?'

'I don't know how I can make this more plain. I am telling you NOTHING. Now excuse me. I have my public to entertain.'

Wilma stood and stared as Barbu disappeared behind the back curtain of the stage. This had been a highly unsatisfactory encounter. She was none the wiser regarding Barbu's involvement in her own story and, even worse, they still had no idea what dastardly deed was about to be perpetrated on the Farside. But at least they now had a decent lead.

'Who do you think the Masked Man is?' she asked, as they pushed their way back out through the tavern.

'I don't know, Wilma,' answered Theodore, frowning deeply. 'But I don't think Barbu knows either. Interesting. It's now more imperative than ever that we manage to get into that ball. And we need to take that poster to Penbert immediately.

Think you're up to all this, Wilma?'

Wilma stared up at her mentor and blinked. 'I do, Mr Goodman. I really do. I may be small, but I'm very determined.'

Of that there is no doubt. Steel yourself, children. If you're going to read on, you'll need courage and a brave heart.

Chapter 7

Penbert was not pleased. 'One item at a time,' she said, pointing towards a sign on the lab wall. 'Those are the regulations. It's against every protocol in the book to analyse two things at once and—'

'Oh, DO be quiet, Penbert,' roared Titus Kooks, the island's forensic scientist. He was dressed in a large, strangely shaped costume, deep red in colour with odd tubes coming out of it at angles. 'What do you think?' he boomed, gesturing towards it. 'It's my outfit for the Ten-Annual Ceremonies. I went as a lung last time so I found the old costume, gave it a lick of paint, stuck a couple of hoses out of it and – chucks your bobbins! – I'm a heart! Pretty good, eh? I'm working up a song to go with it. Want to hear it?'

'Perhaps another time, Titus,' said Theodore. 'I'm afraid we're in something of a rush. It would appear that the Lowside

Criminal Elements are up to their usual tricks. And we haven't a moment to spare.'

'We don't know *what* they're tricksying,' chipped in Wilma, 'but we do think it might have something to do with this.'

She held out the purple poster for Dr Kooks to look at.

Penbert, Dr Kooks's long-suffering assistant, was standing to one side looking very anxious. She was wearing her standard-issue starched white coat, buttoned right up to the neck, and protective goggles over her considerably thick glasses. Beside her stood Kite Lambard, Wilma's headmistress, who had arrived only a few moments before Theodore.

Penbert cleared her throat. 'At this present time I am already conducting an in-depth analysis of some as yet unidentified grey matter discovered on the message in a bottle found by Miss Lambard. I have given her a case number. That means, according to lab rules, that I have to conclude my results on Miss Lambard's case before commencing on another case with a higher number.' She stopped and stared at everyone in the room.

Dr Kooks thought for a moment then, leaning forward, whispered, 'Pass me the case file, Penbert.'

Penbert, looking more than a little agitated, passed her employer the neat blue file she had just created. Clearing his throat and throwing a relaxed smile to everyone in the room, Dr Kooks took a pencil out of one of the hoses poking from his costume, turned it over and used the rubber at the end to erase the number on the file. Penbert clasped a hand suddenly to her mouth. Then, taking a new file, Dr Kooks, still smiling, stuffed the purple poster inside it and wrote the same number he'd just rubbed out from the blue file on its front.

'There you go,' he beamed, handing Penbert the new file with the purple poster inside it. 'That's got a lower number than the blue file now. So that gets analysed first.'

'I hope you don't mind,' said Theodore, turning to Kite, 'but, given the urgency, I think we should take precedence.'

'Absolutely,' replied Kite with a firm nod. 'I don't mind at all. That all right with you, Penbert?'

But Penbert couldn't speak. She'd gone a strange reddish colour around the mouth and was still glaring at Dr Kooks.

'What I need from you, Penbert,' said Theodore, stepping in to diffuse the tension, 'is any information on the ink that's been used. I don't think I've ever seen a colour like it.'

Penbert pushed her goggles up on to her forehead and took a good long look at the ink on the poster. 'Actually,' she said, her brow knitted in concentration, 'I think I've seen something just like this before. I'll have a look under my microscope.' She sat down in front of it, then paused. 'If you could remove your half-eaten bun from my microscope plate first, Dr Kooks,' she said, tight-lipped, 'that would be helpful.'

Lemone stared at the bun as the scientist grabbed it and popped it into a nearby beaker. He looked at his watch. 11 a.m. He hadn't eaten anything in well over an hour. That was the sort of relentless hardship he had to put up with in this job, he thought, as he licked his finger and dipped it in his pocket in the hope of finding a crumb.

Penbert peered closely into her microscope viewer. 'Just as I thought,' she said, making a few scribbled notes. 'It's a highly unusual vermilion ink. It comes from a rare beetle. The widdybug. Fat little thing. Can fly, but with great difficulty. The ink is stored in a pair of sacs just under the wings. Crush them and out it comes.'

'Can you tell us anything more about this beetle?' asked Theodore, reaching for his pipe. 'Its habitat, where it can be found. That sort of thing?'

Penbert shot a short, irritated look at Kooks. 'No. I'm afraid not. I did have a large catalogue of island insects, but Dr Kooks ripped it up to make a papier-mâché opera house.'

'I did!' Kooks bellowed, pointing to a far corner. 'There it is! Took me a whole week!'

'Hmm,' commented Theodore, twitching his moustache. 'No matter. I have an encyclopaedia of island creatures back at Clarissa Cottage. Now then. Miss Lambard's matter. Have you got anything more on that?'

'Well,' Penbert began, blinking rapidly, 'before I was controversially diverted . . . I did find something, yes. The grey matter is a tiny fragment of a piece of lichen. It's an uncommon genus found on damp stone rather than wood. And it only grows in the dark. So wherever this note originated from it's wet and it's probably underground.'

Theodore's eyes widened. 'That's the best breakthrough we've had in years, Kite.'

'I can set to work straight away,' nodded Kite enthusiastically. 'Scout the island, investigate everywhere that might fit the bill. If I take Wilma with me, I can have the island covered in half the time. I know time is of the essence, but could you spare her?'

'Actually, she can pick up our disguises on the way,' said Theodore, nodding. 'And what do we call that, Wilma?'

'Oh, wait,' said the apprentice detective, pulling a rubber Bunsen burner tube from Pickle's mouth. 'It's the thing where you do two things at once. It's called . . . doing two things at once.'

'Killing two birds with one stone,' corrected Theodore. 'So Lemone and I will return home, see what more we can find out about the habitat of the widdybug, and you can head off with Miss Lambard, fetch our disguises for the ball and keep your eyes peeled for any possible locations where Max and Pru may be being held.'

'It'll be quite something if Max and Pru are found after

all these years,' said Kooks, placing a hand on Theodore's shoulder.

The great detective's eyes softened. 'Yes,' he said gently, 'it would. I must confess I had almost given up. When they went missing all those years ago, I searched high and low. My Clue Board was a mass of half-guesses and dead ends. After five years of searching I stopped. I thought it best to accept that they were lost. But now, with Kite's recent discovery, that long-forgotten hope is rekindled.'

'Perhaps they're trapped in a cave?' suggested Wilma. 'Or a cramped, mouldy box? Wherever they are, they're probably near the sea. Otherwise they'd never have managed to get that message out. In the bottle, I mean.'

'It's a great deduction, Wilma,' said Theodore. 'Well! We all know what we have to do. Good luck, everyone!'

Wilma followed Kite towards the door, virtually skipping with delight. Not only was she being given super-responsible jobs to do, but with the discovery of the lichen there was every chance that she was edging closer to unravelling the mystery of her own past. It was SO exciting.

'They didn't give me back my visitor badges,' Penbert whispered, wringing her hands anxiously as she watched them all leave. 'This is the worst day at work I've ever had.'

63

Titus put a comforting arm about her shoulders. 'Chin up, Penbert. I'll make you some more visitor badges. Now how's about I brew one of my special teas?'

Penbert sighed and shoved her glasses up her nose. 'Will it explode again? Like last time?'

Kooks pulled a face. 'It might.'

Racing against time, strange beetles, damp nooks, island in peril? It's all kicking off. Quick, on to the next page, on to the next page!

Chapter 8

'He was ever so striking, wasn't he?' mused Barbu. 'And that mask! SUCH a good look. Maybe I should get myself a costume? Perhaps a cape with zigzag edges? Or a dazzling belt? Or a hat, set at a rakish angle? What do you think?' He looked over at his henchman and apprentice, but they were shuffling awkwardly and staring at their shoes. Barbu gave a small irritated sigh. 'This is my problem. I'm the only one with *vision*. The sooner I meet this Masked Man the better. After being stuck with you two it'll be a *relief* to chat to someone with a scrap of imagination.'

There was a soft knock at the door. Barbu wafted his hand towards it, lay back on the battered chaise longue in their room and closed his eyes. 'Go and see who that is,' he said. 'And if it's the management wanting another show tell them I am creatively indisposed. And then . . . poke them in the eye or something.'

Tully opened the door to reveal a hooded figure standing before him, his face obscured by a heavy woollen cowl that fell heavily over the top of his head and on to his shoulders. 'I have come with information,' the man said in a low, whispering voice. 'Information for Mr D'Anvers.'

Tully turned. 'It's a man in a blanket. He wants to speak to you.'

Barbu opened one eye. 'Man in a blanket? What is this? A sleepover? No chance of that. This room is tiny. Janty's sleeping in a drawer.'

The hooded man pressed his way past Tully into the room. 'I have information that may benefit you, Mr D'Anvers. Perhaps we can come to a mutual arrangement? I can help you and you can help me.'

Barbu sat up and frowned towards the shrouded figure. 'This is all very mysterious. Who are you?'

'I would prefer to remain anonymous for the time being,' said the man with a bow. 'All will be revealed in due course. I come with a great opportunity for the right sort of villain. If you are not the right villain, then I shall take my information elsewhere. But I come to you first. You are, after all, the greatest rogue on the island.'

Barbu shrugged. 'That is true. And it's extremely sensible of you to flatter me. Well, out with it.'

From the shadow of his hood, the man spoke. 'You will be aware that something is afoot on the Lowside of the island . . . something that is being perpetrated by an unknown Masked Man.'

Barbu's eyes narrowed. 'Yes,' he snapped. 'What of it?'

'Everyone wants to know who the Masked Man is and where he can be found.'

'Pfft. I know *that*. Tell me something more interesting or get out.'

'Did you also know that Theodore P. Goodman and all the enforcement officers of Cooper are totally preoccupied with finding him? Which means –' the hooded man stepped a little closer and lowered his voice to a dread hush – 'that the bigger prize is . . . vulnerable.'

'What? What bigger prize?' Barbu hissed, leaning in closer.

Cupping Barbu's ear, the hooded man bent towards the diminutive villain and whispered. Barbu listened, his eyes widening.

'And you think that's actually possible?' he said, frowning with incredulity.

'It's more than possible,' said the man. 'I have the plans to do it.'

Barbu's eyes flashed with excitement. 'I said I needed a horrible plan. And this is it! If I pull this off, Cooper will be on its knees! It's AWFUL! It's SO DASTARDLY! It's BRILLIANT!'

'But it's very important that the Masked Man be helped every step of the way,' whispered the hooded figure. 'To succeed, Theodore P. Goodman must be distracted for as long as possible.'

'Oh, this is perfection!' laughed Barbu. 'And it comes with the added bonus of seeing Theodore P. Goody-Goody Goodman totally humiliated.'

He turned and fixed the hooded man with a firm stare. 'You have yourself a deal. Tully! Glove!'

The thuggish henchman reached into a pocket and pulled out a small, black velvet glove. Taking it, Barbu yanked it on and held out his hand to shake on the deal. 'You have done well. *Now bring me those plans,*' he said, with an evil sneer.

The hooded figure gave a small bow. 'You will hear from me again, Mr D'Anvers. And remember the agreement. You get what you want, but I get what *I* want too. Those are my terms.'

'Yes, yes,' answered Barbu, with a wave of his hand. 'I look forward to our next encounter.'

'Later tonight, after the Villains' Ball, I will come to you. Wait for me behind the Skullduggery Ballroom.' And, with that, the Hooded Figure slipped from the room.

Janty, who hadn't heard what the Hooded Figure had whispered, shut the door and turned to his master. 'What was that about? And what does he want in return?'

Barbu was pacing, his face alight with scheming. 'It doesn't matter what he wants. He's not going to get it. But, by Cooper, our bad luck is about to end! For GOOD!'

And he threw back his head and gave out the worst evil laugh anyone had ever heard.

It's such a shame books don't come with lip-readers, isn't it? Anyone got any ideas about what the Hooded Figure whispered? Anyone? Oh GAH. How ANNOYING.

Chapter 9

'Right then,' said Kite, wheeling out the Academy's tricycle and sidecar. 'You and Pickle can use this. I'll take the booster bike and if we . . . Oh.' She stopped and stared at her only pupil and her dog. 'What are you wearing?'

Wilma had quickly made herself what seemed to be a large and unwieldy cardboard outfit that looked suspiciously like a leaking fountain pen, while Pickle, for safety reasons, had water wings on each leg, a lifejacket round his middle and a small yellow bowler hat perched precariously on his head.

'I had a quick chat with Inspector Lemone,' explained Wilma, pulling down her outfit so that she could peer out of the face hole that hadn't been cut in quite the right place. 'And he said I should go all inky-speck-you-us. I wasn't quite sure what that meant. So I've concentrated on the inky bit.'

Kite blinked. 'I think he meant inconspicuous. That's sort of a different thing. It involves subtlety and trying to go unnoticed.'

'Oh,' said Wilma, a little disappointed. 'So I won't need this outfit then?'

'Probably not . . .'

Wilma screwed her mouth sideways. It was a shame, there was no denying it, but it was most likely for the best. With her pen costume on she couldn't walk, let alone pedal, and she and Pickle did have half the island to cover.

'Super,' continued Kite, pulling a battered leather helmet from her side satchel and putting it on. 'So I'll scout the right side of the island and you scout the left. You'll need to go through the border. All clear?'

Wilma was disentangling one of her plaits from her cardboard costume. 'I think so,' she replied, tugging. 'Just one question – how do I look for damp, underground places when I'm not damp or underground?'

'It's a good question, Wilma,' Kite answered with a nod.

'Have you got an answer to the question?' asked Wilma, after a long pause.

'No,' answered Kite, with a firm shake of her head. 'No, I haven't. Right then,' she added, throwing her leg over the booster bike. 'Let's get cracking.'

The booster bike was a high-seated bicycle with a small rocket device attached to its back axle. Kite pushed down on the starter pedal with her heel and a thick plume of sooty smoke belched out.

'Cheerio!' she yelled, as the rocket burst to life, and off she zoomed, head down and hunched over.

Wilma watched her go then turned towards Pickle. 'Do you think she'll be all right?'

Pickle stared up from under the brim of his yellow bowler hat. He had enough to worry about without adding a maniac headmistress into the mix, so he just gave a short snort and left it at that and as Wilma mounted the saddle he jumped into the sidecar.

Wilma spread a small hand-drawn map across the handlebars. 'I've brought a crayon so we can mark the map at any place we think might be damp or underground. And remember, Pickle! In-conker-speckle-was. Or whatever it is. We must do our scouting as quietly as possible.'

According to Wilma's map, their route would take them west from Coop to That Place Over There, where they would follow the tracks to Is It Nearly Lunch Yet and the Office of the Receiver of Burrowed Things. From there, it was a short journey round the back of the one, small hill, past Hawks Brigade HQ and the Le Poulailler Hotel, then through the poppy fields to Measly Down and the border station. Once into the Lowside, Wilma would have to navigate the Swamp of Heavy Sighs, cycle on to the allotments, go beyond Whiffling Farm in Little Meaning to pass Barbu's seized lair at Rascal Rock and then meet Kite at the disused train line at Uppity Downs on the edge of Filthy Cove.

Wilma, who was small but very determined, knew there was no time to lose. She would speed round, scouting quickly and quietly, making a note on her map of anywhere that might fit the bill. At least that was the plan.

The sky had turned a dull, thick grey and large drops of rain were starting to fall. Squinting into the downpour, Wilma stood up on the pedals to go faster, but as she did so her right foot accidentally knocked the pivoting hitch that joined the sidecar to the tricycle. The locking pin dislodged and, without Wilma noticing, Pickle and the sidecar began to drift away, heading rapidly for the brow of a hill. Pickle blinked in terror, ears flapping manically in the breeze. This was no good. He didn't have a licence to be in control of a sidecar. He had a licence to mix cocktails at Cooper's only nightclub, Shazam. He had a licence to herd geese. He even had a licence to preside over weddings. But sidecars? No.

Then, just as the sidecar was about to hurtle down the hill, its front wheel struck a rock, sending the whole thing skyward. Pickle, who was considerably lighter than the sidecar, felt himself floating up and out of his seat. He could see Wilma, miles beneath him, oblivious to the absence of her constant companion, and as he reached the peak of his ascent, he let out a short, sharp howl. The sidecar clattered to the ground below him while Pickle bounced off the branch of a tree, was catapulted through a washing line and into a rather fetching pink dress, before landing quite sharply back in the sidecar.

Wilma, hearing the commotion at last, looked over her shoulder. 'What the . . . ?' she began, but before she had time to think Pickle and the sidecar sped past her, the beagle yowling as he went.

'Oh no!' cried Wilma, eyebrows shooting upward. 'The sidecar's got no brakes!' Pedalling furiously until she was neck and neck with Pickle and the sidecar, she extended a hand. 'Hold out your paw, Pickle!' she yelled. 'Your paw!'

This was no time for shaking hands, thought Pickle, frowning, when here he was, clattering towards a calamitous end. Perhaps she wanted to say goodbye? A short moment of tenderness by which to remember him? His eyes welled up. Throwing back his head, Pickle howled into the rain. Wilma, realizing she had a matter of moments before they got to the bottom of the hill and met certain disaster, leaned over as far as she could and grabbed at Pickle's paw. As her fingers tightened round him, she pulled hard on the tricycle's brakes, yanking Pickle out of the sidecar just as it rattled over the grassy verge and into the pond before them, sending ducks and geese scattering.

Wilma, panting, lifted Pickle on to the sidebar of the tricycle. 'Well, that was close,' she said, heaving a sigh of relief. 'You'll have to sit here now. Goodness. You're wearing a pink dress. It um . . . no. It suits you.'

Pickle did not respond. He'd had just about enough humiliations for one day, thank you.

The search for the elusive damp underground spot was proving more difficult than Wilma had imagined. So too was the inconspicuous bit. Instead of going unnoticed, Wilma, who wasn't very good at map reading, was stopping every person she encountered, pointing at her hand-drawn map and asking if there were any damp holes nearby, a question that elicited odd looks and suspicion rather than useful information. Conscious that she might not be fulfilling the inconspicuous part of her task, Wilma rectified the situation by simply shouting, 'Just pretend you didn't see me!' as she pedalled off. 'That should do the trick,' she muttered to Pickle, who looked a bit sceptical.

She had almost made her circuit of the left side of the island and was now heading towards the dark turrets of Rascal Rock, the one-time lair of Barbu D'Anvers. It sat perched on a rocky outcrop, connected to the island by the rickety Um Bridge and was shrouded in low cloud and mist. As she rode towards it, she could just make out the figure of a man standing guard. He was a scrawny-looking thing, hair flattened by the rain, and had the sort of face that might have worked better on a mule.

He looked up as he saw Wilma approaching and held his hand up. 'No persons allowed to pass, I'm afraid,' he said. 'Not without a lot of paperwork and official stamps.'

Wilma stopped and, after helping Pickle to the floor, dismounted. She stuck her thumb under her Apprentice Badge and shoved it upward so the man could see it. 'I'm Wilma Tenderfoot,' she explained. 'Theodore P. Goodman's apprentice. I'm scouting for damp holes.'

The man, wiping his wet fringe from his eyes, peered towards the badge then stepped back and thumbed his own badge forward. 'Gerald Mothma. Cooper Office for People Who Owe Loads. The people behind me are the Security Administrators with Notepads and Pens.' He nodded his head towards a group of four people huddled under a large umbrella. 'We're guarding Rascal Rock. What with it being seized and everything.'

'I see,' said Wilma, nodding and pursing her lips to look as official as possible. 'And are you aware of any holes or caves that are damp?'

Gerald shook his head. 'We only stand here. Haven't been inside. No one's allowed inside. Well, no one except Mrs Scrabs.'

'Who's she?' asked Wilma, getting out her apprentice's notebook and licking the end of her crayon.

'Barbu D'Anvers's housekeeper. Or at least she was. When he was living here.'

'Cart coming!' called out one of the group behind them.

Gerald turned and held out a hand to halt the horse-drawn carriage that was trotting slowly towards them. He peered up towards a man in a heavy overcoat and cap.

'Hello, Joe!' he said, waving him through. 'Food delivery cart,' he explained to Wilma, who watched as the cart made its way over Um Bridge. 'Wouldn't like to drive that over the bridge in this weather. Especially with the wind up.'

Wilma frowned. 'That's a lot of food for one person, isn't it?' she said, gesturing towards the heaps of provisions in the back of the cart as it disappeared towards the front entrance. 'Is Mrs Scrabs a large lady with an enormous appetite?'

'Can't say I know,' said Gerald, with a shrug. 'I've never met her. I just stand guard here and make sure none of the Criminal Elements get back in. Not until Barbu D'Anvers has paid off his debts anyhow.'

'Wilma!' called out another voice to their left. Wilma turned and saw Kite on the booster bike spluttering towards them. 'Got to Filthy Cove. Waited for a bit. Thought I'd carry on, meet you up the trail. Find anything?' asked Kite, giving her starter pedal another kick. 'I've not had much luck. Quite hard finding damp places when everything is damp.'

'I haven't found anything either,' said Wilma, with a regretful shake of her head. 'But Pickle has picked up a lovely pink dress. So it's not been a complete waste of time.'

Pickle rolled his eyes.

'All right then,' said Kite, gritting her teeth. 'Best be off. I'll see you back at Clarissa Cottage. And, Wilma,' she shouted, as the bike kangaroo-hopped away, 'don't forget the costumes!'

Wilma's eyes widened. 'The costumes! I'd clean forgotten! If I don't get to the fancy-dress shop before it closes, it will be a catastrophe!'

Pickle's ears pricked. Cat? Where?

'No, Pickle. Catastrophes are nothing to do with cats,' explained Wilma, getting back on the tricycle.

Which was a shame. Onward, brave adventurers! Onward!

Chapter 10

'**W**ell, well,' said Theodore, tapping the page in front of him purposefully with a finger. 'The widdybug only has one natural habitat on Cooper. And that's in blue-cabbage patches. They live in the soil and once a year, during blooming season, they burrow up and fly into the air to mate.'

'Can't bear blue cabbage,' said Lemone, giving the fire a prod with the poker. 'Gives me terrible wind. Absolutely awful. Proper trumpets.'

'I'll bear that in mind,' said Mrs Speckle, Theodore's loyal housekeeper who was, just at that moment, bringing a tray into her employer's study. 'Here you are, Mr Goodman, fresh corn crumbles and a piping pot of peppermint tea.'

Mrs Speckle was the one woman on Cooper you wouldn't want to cross. If you look up the phrase 'no nonsense' in a dictionary, it has a picture of Mrs Speckle next to it. She was fearsome, stubborn and she hated a draught. All her clothes were knitted, including her spectacles and her wellingtons, and she wore two bobble hats at all times in case of cool-breeze-based emergencies. She made the finest corn crumble biscuits on Cooper and nobody, but NOBODY made a tastier pot of peppermint tea.

Inspector Lemone flushed red. He had, for many years, held a deep and uncomplicated love for Mrs Speckle, a bit like a rabbit's unending adoration for the carrot. She was his first thought in the morning and his last thought at night. But he had never told her. What would she, a woman who could bake biscuits and knit cupboards, want with him, a slightly sweaty officer of the law? Nothing, probably. And now that she knew he farted badly when he ate blue cabbage she'd be even less interested in him. This was a *disaster*.

'Thank you, Mrs Speckle,' said Theodore, turning from his reading lectern. A large, heavy book was open on it, with an old battered leather cover and paper worn with age. The great and serious detective ran his finger down the page to a small map in the bottom right-hand corner. 'According to my Cooper Almanac, blue cabbage is only grown in one area. Needs a specific acidity in the soil. And that place is . . .' He peered closer. 'Emued Farm. Hmm. Now where is that?'

Inspector Lemone wasn't listening. He was blinking rapidly

and fingering the edge of his hat anxiously as Mrs Speckle threw some more coals on the fire. 'When I said wind,' he began to mumble, swallowing deeply, 'I didn't mean . . . that is to say . . .'

'It's all right, Inspector,' answered Mrs Speckle, shoving one of her bobble hats up her forehead. 'I have five brothers. Blue cabbage made them all blow like a gale. Right then. I've got a beef bone to grind. Oh, and, Mr Goodman,' she added, as she galumphed towards the door in her knitted wellingtons, 'eat those corn crumbles while they're hot.' And, with that, she was gone.

Theodore was halfway up his bookcase steps, reaching for the Here to There map of Cooper, a handy reference book for finding anywhere on the island. Inspector Lemone, slightly stunned by the exchange with the love of his life, wandered absent-mindedly over to the study desk and reached for the biscuits.

'She called me *Inspector*,' he muttered. 'That was nice, wasn't it? Never been entirely sure she knows who I am. Although that would be odd because I'm here every day. All the same, I've never liked to assume. Mmm. Warm corn crumbles. Delicious.'

'Here it is!' said Theodore, above him. 'Emued Farm. North-east of Hare Forest below the pig poke. Owned by Cicatrise Hurl. He can whistle in seventeen different accents. Very talented fellow,' he added, jumping down to the floor. 'Oh. There don't seem to be any biscuits left. Again.' He stared down at the empty plate.

'Did I eat all of them? Was that me?' asked Lemone, looking around the room to see if anyone else was the culprit.

Theodore looked at his friend and said nothing.

'There's lots of peppermint tea left,' added Lemone, lifting the pot lid to release a small cloud of aromatic steam. 'Shall I pour you one?'

'Don't worry,' answered Theodore, his moustache giving a little twitch, 'I'll do it myself. I am very particular about how I take my tea and, by the looks of it,' he said, peering into the top of the pot, 'it needs to stew for another thirty seconds.'

'Hang on . . .' said Inspector Lemone, pursing his lips in thought. 'Emued Farm. Isn't that where Glenda Blaize's sister, Brenda, runs the Cooper Vegetable School?'

'Yes, indeed,' said Theodore, still staring into the teapot, 'which might give us more leads. She's even got a vegetable museum if I remember correctly. They do box deliveries too. We should go there and ask to see a list of anyone who's had access to that blue-cabbage patch recently. Or ordered a lot of blue cabbage. You never know. Bugs do end up in boxes. Either way, it'll be a good place to start. Well, I think my peppermint tea is ready.'

'Crumbs!' exhaled Kite, as she burst in through the door, dripping. 'Soaked to the skin. It's coming down in sheets out there. Booster bike broke down. Had to push it all the way from Measly Down. Wilma's hot on my heels. She's picking up the costumes from There's Fancy! We're both a bit bedraggled.'

Suddenly a red-faced and very wet Wilma entered the study. She was carrying a large hessian sack bulging with costumes. Pickle, who was also sopping wet, trotted to the middle of the room and with one all-encompassing sneeze, proceeded to shake himself dry, sending muddy, slightly smelly dog spray scattering about the room.

'Ugh, Pickle!' cried out Wilma, scrunching her nose up in disgust and wiping her face clean of stinky dog drops. 'Smells like dead toads.'

'Here,' said Theodore, pouring more tea, 'have a cup of this. It'll warm you up. I've got an interesting lead on the widdybug but what with the First Ceremony and the Villains' Ball tonight, we'll have to leave that till tomorrow. How did you two get on? Find anything useful?'

Kite took a cup and shook her head. 'I'm afraid not,' she answered. 'How about you, Wilma?'

The apprentice detective was standing next to the fire,

wringing the rain out from her pinafore. 'Same here. Didn't find anything much. Although I did discover that Barbu's old housekeeper, Mrs Scrabs, is still living at Rascal Rock and she likes her food.'

'We should probably try again on a drier day,' suggested Kite. 'Sorry, Theodore, it's been a bit of a waste of time.'

The great detective stood a while in thought. 'Nothing investigative is ever a waste of time,' he pondered, reaching for his notebook and making a few scribbles. 'Now then. Costumes for the Villains' Ball. It's only half an hour before we have to be at the First Ceremony so we need to get a move on. What have you got for us, Wilma?'

Wilma frowned. 'The thing is that,' she began, emptying the costumes on to the floor, 'because it's the First Ceremony and everything, there's been a bit of a run on the Costume Shop, so I sort of had to take what they had left. So I'm going in this . . .' She held up a small beige shepherd's costume complete with a tidy blond beard, clay pipe and crook. 'And then I've got this . . .' She held up a woolly suit. 'For Pickle. So he's going as a sheep.' Theodore stifled a small laugh.

Inspector Lemone blinked.

'And then for Miss Lambard and Mr Goodman I managed to get this his and hers outfit.' She bent down and pulled up two sets of leather breeches, puffy sleeved shirts, tri-cornered hats and eye patches. 'So you'll be pirates. I can think up some names for you, if you like? You could be Nasty McNasty,' she said encouragingly to her headmistress. 'And you, Mr Goodman, could be something simple like Mr Pirate. Or Lord Wicked.'

'Lord Wicked's quite good,' said Inspector Lemone, his face brightening. 'What have you got for me? Something terrible and terrifying I hope!'

Wilma's face fell a little and she bit her lip. 'The thing is, Inspector Lemone, they really were running jolly low on costumes and, to make matters worse, the woman who runs the shop is a bit hard of hearing. So I asked for a nasty-crook costume for you.'

'Nasty crook, eh?' smiled Inspector Lemone, giving Theodore a nudge on the arm. 'I'll knock 'em dead!'

'Hmm,' continued Wilma, reaching down for the final costume, 'but I think she misheard me. So, instead, you're going as a pastry cook.' She held up a flowery, flouncy dress with a pinny attached and a cotton bonnet. Theodore gave a light cough and turned away.

Inspector Lemone's smile turned slowly into a small look of despair. 'I'm going to have to go dressed as a woman?' he whispered incredulously.

'Never mind, old man,' said Theodore, giving his colleague

a hearty thump on the back. 'I'm sure you'll be quite the catch.'

Inspector Lemone blinked. Fine, he thought. But there was no way he was going to let Mrs Speckle see him in a dress. NO WAY.

Chapter 11

The rain had finally stopped and the streets were packed. The citizens of Cooper were out in their thousands, lining the pavements in readiness for the Ceremonial Parade. Small tin-pan bands played on corners, wet-cake vendors sang out, side tents with Lantha tournaments were full to bursting and fragrant pink blossom blew gently from mood dispensers overhead. Wilma had never seen such a crowd and, despite the seriousness of the job before them, she felt a frisson of excitement.

'Wish I could enter the Lantha contest,' said Inspector Lemone, raising a rueful eyebrow in the direction of the brightly striped awnings. 'Quite fancy my chances.'

Wilma said nothing. She had played Inspector Lemone at Lantha, Cooper's favourite board game, every evening since arriving at Clarissa Cottage and he was yet to beat her. In fact, he was yet to beat anyone. Even Pickle, who inevitably just sat chewing the counters, was better than him.

It is a general truth that adults finding themselves in anything approaching a carnival atmosphere take leave of their senses. Everywhere Wilma looked, grown men were wearing hats shaped like tankards while ladies had hitched up their skirts and were blowing on pip-nuts, a small shell-like husk that when blown properly emitted a deep and resonant bellow. Some people were dancing, others were singing and one man, so beside himself with joy, simply stood on the spot and bounced up and down with his arms in the air.

'They wouldn't be so happy if they knew what we know,' whispered Lemone, reaching for a free wet cake.

'And we don't know much,' answered Wilma.

Glenda Blaize was waiting with Melba Toest, Captain Brock and the men of the 2nd Hawks Brigade at the back of the National Museum, with the floats that were readying for the parade.

'Ho there!' called out Captain Brock as Theodore and the others approached. 'No citizens permitted in this area!'

'It's all right,' answered Theodore, lifting his eye patch. 'It's me – Detective Goodman. We're in disguise.'

'So you are,' beamed Captain Brock, stepping forward to shake the detective's hand. 'Would never have known it's you. What's the story?'

Theodore reached into a pouch tied to his large leather belt and pulled out the poster for the Villains' Ball. 'Seen this?' he asked, holding it out for Captain Brock to look at. 'We intend to infiltrate the Criminal Elements tonight, after the ceremony, and try to find out what they're planning.'

'So you don't think they'll strike during this ceremony then, Mr Goodman?' asked Glenda Blaize, peering over Captain Brock's shoulder.

Theodore raised one eyebrow. 'I can't rule it out, Madam Cooperate, but I think it's unlikely. We think this Villains' Ball might be some sort of rallying point. A gathering of the ruthless, if you will. It seems this Masked Man, the mastermind behind the ball, is the one we're looking for. But, as to who he is, your guess is as good as ours.'

'Though we have found out about a beetle,' piped up Wilma.

'She's right,' said Theodore, casting a glance down at his young apprentice. 'The ink on the poster comes from the widdybug. It lives in blue-cabbage patches. They grow it over at Emued Farm, where your sister works, I believe. We're going to head over there in the morning.'

Glenda rolled her eyes. 'You'll need the patience of a saint, Mr Goodman,' she advised. 'My sister's a bit highly strung. Gets a bee in her bonnet and who knows where it'll lead. She'll be happy to help you though, I'm sure.'

'Sounds as if you should be concentrating all your efforts on finding this Masked Man, Mr Goodman,' said Dromley Abbams, creeping forward. 'If I can offer my services, I would be happy to be of assistance in any way I can. If Madam Cooperate can spare me, of course. My official duties must be honoured first.'

'Oh, don't go on, Dromley,' snapped Glenda. 'Nobody's interested. I think Mr Goodman is perfectly capable of sorting out this mess by himself.'

Behind them, crowds of people in ornate costumes were climbing up on to their floats for the parade. There was a float celebrating the animals of Cooper, a float for cakes, a float that consisted entirely of people dressed as slightly misshapen and inconvenient furniture, a float that shot Sugarcane Swizzle fizz from siphons and a float in the shape of the One Small Hill scattered with goats and rabbits and, rather ominously, a wolf. Beyond those, Wilma could just make out a much grander display. A golden podium was being winched into place and attendants, dressed in luxurious livery, were being helped up on to the platform around it.

'That's for the Grand Tombola,' whispered Inspector Lemone, spotting Wilma straining to see. 'Very too-ra-loo,' he added, his eyes widening.

'Can I help you, miss?' asked Captain Brock, stepping

forward. 'If you're for the Embroidery Float, then that's over there, to the right.'

Inspector Lemone fixed Captain Brock with a hard, penetrating stare. 'It's me, Brock,' he mumbled from the corner of his mouth. 'Lemone.'

The leader of the 2nd Hawks Brigade stood for a moment in open-mouthed silence. Sometimes, when one finds oneself in an awkward situation, it's best just to clear the throat and pretend nothing has happened. Which is precisely what Captain Brock did. 'Are you ready, Madam Cooperate?' he asked, turning swiftly from Inspector Lemone. 'If you take your place, the parade can start.'

'And so it begins,' declared Glenda Blaize, as she was helped up on to the Ceremonial Float, Melba Toest at her side. 'The Grand Tombola is secured. Pass me the Bell of Liberty. As its peals ring out, let the rituals commence!'

A large golden bell on a plump red cushion was lifted up towards Glenda. A reverential hush fell over the crowds as the Cooperate General, standing tall and proud, took it by its handle, held it aloft and rang the bell loud and clear.

A great cheer went up from the parade floats, cheers that were heard and echoed by the people standing outside the museum's gates. Hats were tossed into the air and flocks of silver starlings were released from golden cages.

At last the gates to the museum were opened. Wilma gasped at the crowd of people outside them, stretching back as far as the eye could see. The people at the front waved small commemorative flags handed out at the gate, while those at the back used handheld periscopettes to see over the heads of those in front. It was a swirling mass of faces and sounds while over it all the pump-air fantasma-organ on the lead float blasted out grand and luxurious tunes. To Wilma it seemed as if every man, woman and child on Cooper — even the lowside ones — was cheering with delight. She had never experienced anything like it. The floats exited through the museum gates and on to the streets, the crowds flooding around and behind them, moving in the same direction as the procession.

'Stay close to Miss Lambard and myself, Wilma,' shouted Theodore over the din, 'and keep your eyes peeled. Anything suspicious, let me know.'

Wilma nodded and looked down at Pickle. He seemed uncharacteristically nervous. Perhaps it was the sheer size of the crowd? Or perhaps it was because, now he was dressed as a sheep, he was being eyed hungrily by the wolf on the Animal Float. Wilma stared up. She was certain there'd been some rabbits on that float. Not any more there weren't. She decided to play it safe, bent down and picked up her beagle.

'Come on, Pickle,' she whispered into his tatty ear. 'Let's go.'

The procession was moving at walking pace so it wasn't hard for Wilma to keep up, but the depth and intensity of the crowds made it difficult to work out whether anyone was being suspicious. Suddenly, from the corner of her eye, Wilma spotted Tully pushing his way through the hordes. Behind him was Barbu, who was staring up at Glenda Blaize, and following him was Janty, who was scribbling frantically into a notebook. Wilma frowned. They were clearly up to something. But what?

Wilma called out, 'Mr Goodman!' but the noise and atmosphere meant she had to shout again. 'MR GOODMAN!' At last he looked over his shoulder at her. 'Barbu D'Anvers is here,' she yelled, trying to be heard. 'He's over there,' she gestured with her head, 'pushing his way through the crowd. I think he's trying to keep up with the Grand Ceremonial Float.'

Theodore, straining to hear his young apprentice, nodded and peered into the crowd in the direction she had indicated. He could just see Tully's head, but his line of sight was impeded, preventing him from pinpointing his nemesis.

He turned and called towards Lemone. 'D'Anvers is in the crowd over there somewhere,' he shouted. 'Follow him and see if you can work out what he's up to. I'll continue my watch for the masked man. Just in case.'

Lemone nodded and trotted off obediently in the direction of the Ceremonial Float, teetering slightly in his heels. 'Make way!' he shouted, in a high squeaky voice. 'Pregnant lady! Pregnant lady coming through!'

Wilma, adrenaline pumping through her, strained on tiptoes to try to see where Janty had got to and what he was doing. The Detective Top Tips were quite clear that creeping around after suspects produced results. It was probably a massive clue. But *to what*? Frustrated by her lack of height and struggling with Pickle in her arms, Wilma looked at the float to her left to see if there was anything on which she and Pickle could perch to get a bit higher. They wouldn't be able to jump up on to the float, that would draw too much attention to them, but an extra few inches would make looking out for suspiciousness a lot easier.

The parade was nearing the Central Plaza and Wilma could just make out the Ceremonial Platform where the Grand Tombola would be placed. She had to think quickly! Just above her, on the float, there was a large metal ring. Reaching up with one arm and holding Pickle in the other, she swung herself up on to a small ledge that ran the length of the low, long platform that formed the base of the float, placing Pickle down in front of her.

'That's better. Right, Pickle, what can you see?' she said, searching the crowd with her eyes.

Half a sausage to the left. A bread crust to the right. Never mind suspects, thought Pickle, drooling. This was the important stuff.

Wilma strained to see deeper into the crowd. There they were! Barbu was shouting at Janty who was tucking his notebook into a knapsack. Suddenly Barbu struck Janty sharply across the ear. Wilma gasped. Just behind them, she could see Inspector Lemone wading through the crowd, trying to get closer to the villainous trio. Men were tipping their hats at him while one woman seemed to be following him with a small chair and encouraging him to sit down.

And then Wilma saw him.

Over the crowds, in the Central Plaza, to the right of the Ceremonial Platform, a man in long boots and a frock coat was nailing something to the trunk of the old oak tree. Wilma narrowed her eyes. He turned briefly in her direction, casting a look over his shoulder. He was wearing a mask! Wilma's mouth fell open. Leaping down from the ledge, Wilma barged over to Mr Goodman. 'The Masked Man! I've seen him! By the old oak! He's banging up a poster!'

Captain Brock, whose job it was to spot many things at once, came rushing over, Kite close behind.

'Quickly,' shouted Theodore. 'We must catch him before he gets away!'

'We'll have to try to push through the crowd,' shouted Captain Brock.

But the crowd, excited by the arrival of the Grand Tombola

in the Central Plaza, seemed bigger and more impenetrable than ever. With Captain Brock leading the way, Theodore, Kite and Wilma tried to press through the ever-increasing masses as quickly as they could. But it was a near impossible task, like swimming against the tide.

'Clear a way there!' Wilma could hear Captain Brock shouting.

But it was no use. The organ was playing ever louder behind them and the cheers from the crowds were at fever pitch.

Then at last Wilma realized they were almost there! The old oak, the tree that had stood in the Central Plaza for hundreds of years, loomed high above them.

Captain Brock turned and shouted over his shoulder. 'I see him, Goodman! I can see him!'

But Theodore was busy trying to disentangle himself from two fellows merry on squifty juice who had him by the shoulders and were trying to get him to turn round and go back with them. Kite barged through and, taking Theodore's arm, pulled him away. If only they could all move quicker! Wilma thought. This was torture!

And then, without warning, Captain Brock appeared above the crowd. He'd climbed up a post box and was now only a short jump away from the old oak where Wilma could still just make out the Masked Man. Captain Brock almost had him!

'Grab him, Brock!' yelled Theodore, catching up as fast as he could.

The leader of the 2nd Hawks Brigade leaped towards the oak tree, but, as he did so, the Masked Man turned. Seeing his pursuer, he reached quickly into a pouch and threw something to the ground. A huge plume of smoke rushed skyward. The crowd gasped. The smoke billowed towards Wilma, making her cough and splutter. When the smoke cleared, the Masked Man had vanished.

'Blast it!' yelled Captain Brock. 'He got away!'

'Smoke bomb,' coughed Theodore, as he caught up, reaching for a handkerchief in his pocket and handing it to Kite. 'Put that over your mouth and nose. It'll dissipate soon.'

Wilma, flapping a hand in front of her to clear the smoke, suddenly heard Pickle barking to her left. In all the commotion she had completely forgotten about him. She could just see the beagle, still sitting on the ledge of the float. He was pointing his snout upward and yowling. Still choking, she followed his gaze until she suddenly saw, on the top branch of the old oak, clambering towards the nearby rooftops, the Masked Man!

'Mr Goodman,' Wilma yelled. 'Quick! Look! He's up there!' But, once more, it was too late. He was over the rooftops and out of sight.

Cursing under his breath, Theodore walked over to the poster nailed to the old oak and ripped it down. 'Here it is again. The Villains' Ball.'

'And here's Inspector Lemone,' said Kite, seeing a cotton bonnet bobbing its way towards them through the crowd.

'Sorry, Goodman,' the inspector panted. 'Almost had Barbu, but he and his crew slipped away. On the plus side, I have been given a couple of knitted Babygros. And a tankard of Heavy Ale. Good for breast-feeding, I'm told.'

'Here,' said Captain Brock, bending down to pick up the broken pieces from the smoke bomb. 'These might be useful.'

Theodore took the shattered bits from him and took a closer look. 'Wafer glass,' he said. 'Breaks very easily. Light to carry. Often used in theatres.' He frowned and lifted his palm to his nose. He took a deep sniff. 'Distinctive smell. But I can't quite place it. Wilma, bag this, please. It's a vital clue.'

The young apprentice, who had reclaimed Pickle from the float, took the remnants of the bomb and put them proudly in her bag. This had been her first proper chase in her capacity as a detective-in-training and she couldn't lie – it'd been a thrill. And, what was even better, it wasn't over yet!

'Right then,' said Theodore, casting a look up at Glenda Blaize, who was presiding over the placing of the Grand

Tombola. 'Everyone got their breath back? Then on we go! He may have escaped over the rooftops, but we know where he's headed. To the Villains' Ball!'

Come on, reader! Hurry up! It's a massive chase. And no one's been caught yet. There's not a moment to lose!

Chapter 12

The Skullduggery Ballroom was a large domed building east of the village of Much Mithering. Once a thriving hub of fun and larks for Lowsiders, its former glories were now faded. Ivy crept up the pillars, threatening to swallow the ballroom's dome, and crumbled masonry lay scattered about the ground. Dreary music moaned softly from inside and a dingy light wept out from dirty windows.

A queue of ruffians and scoundrels was waiting to be admitted. A woman was standing at the bottom of a stone staircase that led up to the front doors. In front of her there was a thick green rope between two faded brass stanchions and in her hand a crumpled list. Her hair was piled high into a tight, precise swirl and she wore an ankle-length black velvet gown, pinched at the waist and adorned with a collar of ornate silver ivy.

'Remember we need to convince her that we're Criminal

Elements,' said Theodore. 'Kite, you and I can take the names of the Gnaarl twins. They're still in jail, so there's no chance that they're already here. Wilma, have a quick look through your Clue Ring and pick a suitable name. Lemone, I'm not sure what we can call you.'

'You could be Melanie Getrots,' chipped in Wilma, who was flicking through her Clue Ring at speed. 'She was that pastry poisoner in the Case of the Flung Flan. That would go with your costume . . .'

'Good thinking, Wilma,' whispered Theodore, giving his apprentice a light pat on the back. 'Once we're inside, let's split up. I don't want anyone to do anything foolish – it's far too dangerous – but we need information on that Masked Man. Now, remember, it's vitally important that everyone keep their true identity concealed. So stay in character!'

Wilma nodded. There were only a few people between her and the green rope. She quickly decided to assume the identity of a minor villain from her employer's past, Phoebe Stynk, now locked up, who had once mistakenly kidnapped a poodle thinking it was the effeminate son of a Farside millionaire but was first and foremost the island's worst ever sheep rustler. Pickle was dressed as a sheep and slightly smelt like a sheep. Wilma nodded to herself. She could get away with this. A sheep rustler would definitely choose a sheep-related costume for a costume ball – perfect!

Theodore and Kite were first to the line monitor. 'Names?' asked the monitor, not even bothering to look up.

'Sam and Pam Gnaarl,' answered Theodore, in a low, gruff voice.

The woman checked her list and unhooked the green rope. 'In you go. Next.'

Lemone teetered forwards. 'Melanie Getrots,' he squeaked in as high a voice as he could muster.

The line monitor looked up. 'Melanie Getrots?' she asked, eyes narrowing. 'I thought you were dead?'

Inspector Lemone stood, dithering momentarily, and then, after a sharp poke in the backside from Wilma, blurted, 'No. Not dead. Just a bit lazy.'

The woman frowned. 'Hmm. Well. OK. Up the stairs please. Next.'

Wilma gulped. She absolutely, positively could not afford to muck this up. She shoved Pickle forward with her foot.

'Phoebe Stynk,' she said, concentrating on pulling her ugliest face.

The line monitor stood back and took a good long look at her. 'Bit short for a Criminal Element, aren't you?'

Wilma blinked. 'Legs eaten by crows,' she answered, with a confident nod.

The line monitor registered a small look of surprise and then cast another suspicious look at Pickle. 'What's that?'

she asked, pointing with a long, bony finger.

'Sheep,' answered Wilma. 'Really rotten he is. Proper black sheep.'

'He's white.'

'Grrrrrnnnaaaaaaaaaaar,' Wilma replied, pulling her evilest face to date.

The line monitor raised her eyebrows and gave a small, exasperated sigh. 'All right, go in. But don't let your sheep eat any of the decorations.' And, with that, she lifted the green rope and let Wilma and Pickle pass.

Inside the Skullduggery Ballroom it was chaos. Rogues and villains were swigging bottles of squifty juice, swinging from chandeliers, pulling paintings from walls, dragging statues from their plinths and generally behaving very badly indeed. Wilma gulped. Although she'd had some experience of the odd Criminal Element here and there, it was a different matter entirely to be slap bang in the middle of them. It was like being inside a hornet's nest.

At the far end of the ballroom, a miserable-looking quartet was playing on a raised platform, dodging the odd thrown bottle and grinding out dismal dirges. In front of them, hanging from a hook, was a small hand-drawn sign that read:

REKWESTS. ONE GROGGLE

Wilma watched as a drunken man in a striped hat wobbled over to the stage and threw the band a coin.

'"Cooper Nod"!' he was shouting. 'Play "The Cooper Nod"!'

The band leader, a man with a face so weary it was amazing he was upright, turned and gave a small exhausted signal to his colleagues and, as the familiar opening bars of the island's favourite song struck up, a great cheer filled the room. People all over the hall began to take partners and form lines.

Wilma, mindful of the job before her, dodged through the revellers to a spiral staircase that snaked up the wall to her left. Climbing to the halfway point, she had a clear view of the whole room. This would be a brilliant place to try to spot the Masked Man. In the far corner, she could see Theodore and Kite. They'd taken up places in readiness for the dance. Just below her she could see Inspector Lemone's cotton bonnet. He was looking around anxiously and swaying slightly to the music. Wilma's eyes widened. Tully was striding towards him! He'd obviously recognized the inspector and was about to unmask him! She gripped the rail of the staircase in terror and leaned over to warn the inspector. But she was too late.

'Excuse me,' said Tully gruffly. He cleared his throat. Inspector Lemone spun towards him, clearly terrified. 'I . . . wonder if you would do me the honour of partnering me in this dance.'

Wilma looked down at Pickle in astonishment as Inspector Lemone baulked.

What to do? He couldn't say no. That might cause a scene and blow his cover. But how was he going to dance in these shoes? And with Tully of all people? Oh well. He'd have to go along with it. In for a penny, in for a pound. Pulling his bonnet further down his forehead, Inspector Lemone pursed his lips and, batting his eyelashes, said, 'Much obliged, I'm sure. Although I am breaking in new shoes. I might tread on your toes.'

Tully blinked with mild adoration. 'I don't mind,' he grinned. 'Pretty little thing like you – I wouldn't even feel it.'

'Ha ha ha,' giggled Inspector Lemone. 'You silver-tongued *rogue*.' And with that he punched Tully in the arm.

'Ow. Pretty AND strong,' said Tully, rubbing his arm gleefully. 'This is my lucky day.'

Wilma clamped a hand over her mouth to stop herself from laughing, and looked out over the dancing throng. Criminal Elements without partners were standing round the edges of the room, clapping and singing along, while in the centre of the room, the lined formations moved in time with the music. Pickle sniffed at the air, sensing the presence of a large unattended buffet table. No one would suspect a small wandering sheep. If he played this carefully, he might pull off the food heist of the century. There was a heaving plate of sausages down there. He'd be the stuff of legends!

Wilma scanned the room methodically, searching among the sea of cheering faces for any glimpse of the Masked Man. But he hadn't shown himself yet. She could see Barbu though, scowling in the far corner. Janty was at his side and, not far from them, Theodore and Kite were edging slowly closer, no doubt trying to keep an eye on the rotten rascal. Janty looked miserable, Wilma thought. His head was down and he was scuffing at the floor with his plimsolls. She gave out a small, exasperated sigh at the sight of him. Janty had been nothing but rude to her since their first meeting, but Wilma knew there was good in him. She just knew it. She hoped he'd get a chance to prove it one day, just as Mr Goodman had given her a chance to do the same.

The last chorus of 'The Cooper Nod' was playing at full pelt and the voices of the island's Criminal Elements swelled below her but, just as the final chords were reaching their crescendo, the lights in the ballroom were suddenly extinguished. The music ground to a halt and the singing turned to shouting and angry calls for the lights to come back on. Without warning, a single bright blue light appeared in the middle of the ceiling above them. Wilma cast her eyes upward and there, hanging from a rope that had been lowered through the skylight, lantern in hand, was the Masked Man.

'Thank you for coming!' he yelled as a hush descended on the room. 'The time of the Lowsider is upon us! For too long the Farsiders have had it all their own way! In two days' time, the new Cooperate General will be announced! Another Farsider!'

A large groan rippled through the crowd below.

'But, while the Farsiders may think they are getting what they want, WE shall be taking what we want. Who will rise up with me and help me liberate the riches of our neighbours? The poor shall be poor no more and we shall all live as equals! Are you with me, Lowsiders? Are you with me?'

The hall roared with cheering.

'Then I need your help! With all the Farsiders at the Final Naming Ceremony, every bank, vault and store will be left unattended. We shall take everything from them!'

The Criminal Elements couldn't believe their ears. This was clearly the best idea ever!

'Excuse me!' called out one voice. Pushing his way through the party guests so that he was illuminated by the light above, Barbu came into view. 'You'll probably be needing me! I'm *really* evil! Perhaps we can talk? Come to some arrangement? Seems silly to involve everyone. It's an organizational nightmare.'

'My plan is for all Lowsiders!' called down the Masked Man.

'But—' Barbu began.

107

'I shall come again!' the Masked Man shouted. 'The less said till the last minute the better – it makes us harder to stop. But be ready for me!' And, with that, he dropped a glass ball from his belt. It fell to the ground and up swelled an explosion of yellow smoke. The place was in uproar. Wilma, because she was higher placed, could just see over the smoke plume as the Masked Man disappeared back up through the skylight. When she turned and looked out again over the party-goers she realized Barbu and Janty were gone too.

'Oh, what to do?' she whispered, glancing down towards Pickle. 'What the . . . ?' began the young apprentice. 'Where's Pickle?'

Well, we all know where Pickle is. Snaffling that plate of sausages. He's no fool, reader. If there is one rule cast in stone, it's this – when confusion descends, raid the buffet.

Chapter 13

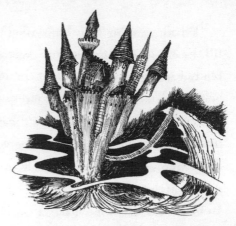

Wilma scrabbled down the stairs as fast as she could. The place was in utter chaos. Fired up by the appearance of the Masked Man, the Criminal Elements were running riot. Bottles were flying through the air, curtains were aflame and everywhere Wilma looked, vicious fights were breaking out and chairs were being launched. Feeling anxious, Wilma ran towards Theodore and Kite, who were standing by the refreshments table.

'Where's Melanie Getrots?' asked Kite, scanning the room. 'I hope she's all right.'

'Here she comes,' yelled Wilma, ducking as a large pie rotated at speed over her head. 'She's with Tully!'

Inspector Lemone, in his disguise as the dread pastry cook, was being escorted through the swarm by Barbu D'Anvers's brainless henchman. 'Watch it!' yelled Tully, shoving an unshaven man firmly in the chest. 'Lady coming through!'

'Thank you, Mr Tully,' squeaked Lemone, fluffing his bonnet. 'I'll be fine now I'm with my companions. Most kind of you to see me across the floor.'

Tully stood for a moment and gulped. 'My pleasure, miss,' he said, with a gentle bow. 'If you'd care to step out for a pie or a squifty juice sometime, then I'd be very glad to escort you again.'

Wilma, Mr Goodman and Kite all looked busily in other directions.

Inspector Lemone gave a short, light cough. 'Oh, don't worry,' he squealed, pursing his lips. 'You'll be seeing me again. Of that you can be sure!'

Tully beamed and gestured towards the back of the hall. 'Better get back to my master. Well, goodbye then.' And off he went, skipping all the way.

'Nobody say a word,' said Lemone, in his normal voice. 'Not ONE word.'

'Under the table,' said Theodore, holding up the long cloth that covered it. 'Then we can talk freely.'

Wilma dropped down on to her knees and crawled into the confined space. Pickle rolled in after her, looking bloated and a bit cross-eyed with joy. 'I'll speak to you later,' she whispered crossly, as Kite, Lemone and Theodore clambered in after them. 'Polishing off grub while you're supposed to be on duty. Honestly, Pickle.'

Yes, thought Pickle. He was on duty. And his duty was to eat as many sausages as possible.

'Right,' began Theodore, shoving his eye patch up on to his forehead. 'We know now what the plan is. But quite how we're going to protect every potential target on the Farside is beyond me.'

'At least we know what the target is though, Mr Goodman,' whispered Wilma, with some enthusiasm. 'It's EVERYWHERE.'

'And everywhere is impossible for us and Captain Brock to monitor,' said Kite. 'At least, I think it is. If you use maths. Which was never my strongest subject, I must confess.'

'It's quite clear,' continued the great and famous detective, 'that what we need to do is concentrate our efforts on uncovering the identity of the Masked Man so we can stop this at the source. So. What do we know?'

'He's good at climbing trees and ropes, he likes a big, smoky bang and he hates the Farside,' said Wilma, reaching for her apprentice's notebook and licking the end of her pencil. 'And he's not afraid of heights.'

'I'd have fainted,' said Lemone, with a shudder. 'All that way up. Nothing but a rope. Hideous.'

'He's got some crazy notions as well,' added Kite. 'All that business about taking what's theirs. I mean, he has got a point. It's not right that Lowsiders are left out of the Ten-Annual Election but Lowsiders not being able to take part in the election and Lowsiders being justified in robbing the Farside blind seem to be two very different things to me.'

'He's an idealist,' nodded Theodore. 'There's no doubt about that. I suspect this chap might even be a decent fellow with good intentions, but he's going about things the wrong way.'

'Can't we just ask Glenda Blaize to not do the ceremonies?' asked Wilma, tapping her pencil on her bottom lip to look efficient. 'What's that thing? She could post a bone.'

Bone? Pickle's ears pricked. What bone? Where?

'Postpone,' corrected Theodore. 'I'm afraid that's impossible. Once the Ceremonial Bell has been rung, there can be no turning back. The tombola is in place. Tomorrow the names will be placed in it and, the day after, a name must be drawn. It's the law.'

'If he is a good person, Mr Goodman,' continued Wilma, 'then maybe when we find him you could ask him to stop being so silly. Like when you tell me to stop trying to break the record for hopping on one foot.'

'But even if we did find him,' said Lemone, kicking away an unconscious villain who had suddenly flopped under the table, 'I doubt if asking him to call everything off is going to do any good. The Criminal Elements are stirred up now. This is a potentially disastrous situation.'

112

'I fear you may be right, Lemone,' said Theodore, his moustache twitching, 'though we don't know what his final plans are yet. But neither do the Criminal Elements. So we must at least try. I fear we are too late to find him tonight, but tomorrow is a new day and we have our lead with the blue cabbage to follow up. We shall arise at dawn's first light. We still have forty-eight hours. There is hope yet! Now I suggest we get out of here while we still can.'

'Oh blast,' said Lemone, as they all crawled back out from under the table. 'Got a ladder in my tights.'

Barbu and Janty had taken advantage of the chaos to creep out through a service door at the rear. They came out into a small, dark alleyway that led away from the Skullduggery Ballroom and into the open fields beyond. Panting, Barbu looked up towards a noise on the tiles above them. It was the Masked Man!

'Here,' he shouted up, holding out a hand. 'Let me help you down. It's me. From inside just now. I'm awful. I can do Chinese burns and everything. Well, my henchman does them for me. Obviously.'

The Masked Man, who was now clinging on to a drainpipe, looked down and took Barbu's hand. 'Thanks,' he called, leaping to the ground. 'I'll be honest,' he added, flattening his frock coat, 'I'm a bit new to this game. Haven't really donc anything like this before.'

Barbu's eyes flashed. 'Oh, really,' he smarmed. 'You'd never know. You've taken to rottenness VERY well.'

'Thanks,' said the Masked Man, smiling. 'Although I don't really want to be properly rotten. Just even things out a bit, you know?'

'I understand,' said Barbu, lying. 'Still, I'm delighted to be able to offer my services. Seeing as it's your first time plotting a fiendish plan and everything. In fact, if you want, you can leave all the arrangements to me. Why don't we meet at the Twelve Rats' Tails tomorrow? I'll finalize the plans for you. That way, you can concentrate on just being MARVELLOUS.'

Janty rolled his eyes.

'Oh, all right then!' answered the Masked Man after a pause. 'I did want to have a go myself, but I'll confess I am a bit unsure about the whole "making it happen" bit. I'm good at speeches and things but I've never organized a mass robbery of half an island before. Well, best be off. Important not to stay in one place for too long. See you tomorrow then.'

'Yes,' said Barbu, casting a quick glance over his shoulder, 'you never know who is lurking. But, before you go, what did you say your name was again . . . ?' He turned back round and coughed. 'Oh. He's gone already. And what's all this smoke?'

'Set off another smoke bomb and vanished into the darkness, master,' said Janty, with a sniff.

Barbu stared into the black of the night to try to catch another glimpse, but it was no good – the Masked Man was already long gone. 'Wasn't he LOVELY,' he mooned. 'SUCH a nice villain.'

'Mr D'Anvers,' said another voice, creeping out from the gloom. 'I hope you haven't forgotten OUR arrangement?'

Barbu twisted on his heels to find himself face to face with the strange, hooded figure from the Inn. 'Oh,' he sneered, 'it's you again. No. I haven't forgotten. Have you brought me those plans?'

The hooded figure reached deep into his cassock and pulled out a tightly rolled bundle of paper. 'Everything you need, Mr D'Anvers,' he replied, handing them over.

Barbu gave them straight to Janty. 'Here. You'll need to start working on those immediately. So get to it. And as for you,' he said, turning back to the hooded man, 'don't creep up on me so much. You're like a bout of indigestion.'

The hooded figure made a small gentle bow. 'Just so long as you keep your end of the bargain, Mr D'Anvers. That is all I ask.' And with a twitch of his cassock he retreated back into the shadows.

'Ugh,' said Barbu, with a small shiver, 'so *needy*. Right then,

Janty. To the Twelve Rats' Tails. The quicker you start work on those plans the better.'

But what are the plans for? WHAT ARE THEY FOR? And that to one side, EVERYBODY knows giving plans to a known villain spells DISASTER.

(You might want to put on some sort of hard hat.)

Chapter 14

A low fog hung in the valley that morning. Goodman and Lemone pedalled away on the tandem while Wilma and Pickle sat in their trailer at the back, huddled together to keep out the cool of the damp morning air. Frost tinged everything with a crystal glow and as the tandem sped onward Wilma could make out hundreds of spider webs in the hedgerows, preserved for a few hours at least in icy splendour.

'There you go,' said Theodore, gesturing towards a slightly dilapidated sign. 'Emued Farm.'

The path towards the old stone farmhouse was in a ramshackle state – strewn with large potholes, a fallen tree and the remnants of a rusty plough abandoned on the verge. A brook ran along one side of the path, framed by bramble bushes and on the other side was a large overgrown meadow.

The front yard sloped up towards the main house. A large

oblong greenhouse ran up the centre of the yard, and beyond it was another wobbly-looking sign that pointed towards the Strangely-shaped-vegetable Museum, one of the great attractions of Cooper Island. Wilma helped Pickle out from the trailer as Lemone and Mr Goodman pulled off their bicycle clips.

A small window opened above them. Out of it popped the head of an odd, slightly dishevelled-looking woman. Her hair was all over the place, and she had dark, streaky smudges on her face.

'The museum's not open till the shadow on that long-hand bit points to that sticky-out bit,' she shouted down, gesturing towards a large sundial set into the wall. 'And watch out for the goat. He can be a bit bumpy.'

Wilma looked around the courtyard. So far, no goat.

'Are you Brenda Blaize?' called up Theodore, shielding his eyes from the morning sun. 'I'm Theodore P. Goodman. I'm conducting an investigation for your sister. We'd like to talk to someone about blue cabbage.'

The woman leaned forward and peered down. 'So you are,' she replied, recognizing him. 'I'm afraid I'm not quite up yet. You'll have to speak to Farmer Hurl. He'll probably be in the kitchen having breakfast.'

'Oooh,' said Lemone, brightening. 'Breakfast? Jolly good.'

*

The farmhouse kitchen was a toasty affair. A wood-burning stove gave off a reassuring heat and the smell of just-baked bread hung in the air. A heavy, wooden table sat in the middle of the room, around which were scattered assorted chairs. A large mug of tea, quietly steaming, was placed on one of them. Standing at the table and rifling through a messy pile of papers was a square-jawed man in a checked shirt and green waistcoat. He wore riding boots and gave off the impression that if he were to kiss a lady, medical assistance would be required. Gosh, he was handsome.

'Aren't you Theodore P. Goodman?' he asked, glancing up casually as they all came in through the back door. 'Detective chap? And who's this?' he added, shooting a dazzling smile in Wilma's direction. 'Other than the prettiest little girl in all of Cooper.'

Wilma blushed. Nobody had ever called her pretty before. She didn't quite know what to do, so she blinked a lot and twirled the ball of her foot into the floor.

'That's my apprentice, Wilma Tenderfoot,' Theodore explained, extending a hand for shaking. 'Hope you don't mind the intrusion. We've got some questions about blue cabbage. Are you Cicatrise Hurl?'

'The very same,' grinned the handsome man, gripping

119

Theodore's hand firmly. 'Blue cabbage? You'll want to talk to Brenda about that. She looks after all the vegetable patches. Don't like to get my hands too dirty, you know.'

'I'm actually more interested in the cabbage-loving widdybug,' Theodore continued, taking his pipe from his pocket and lighting it. 'Apparently you can make ink with them.'

'Yup,' nodded Cicatrise. 'I know. Got pots of the stuff out in the work shed. Mouse makes it.'

'Mouse?' asked Theodore, frowning slightly.

'Yard lad,' explained the dashing farmer, taking a large gulp from his mug. 'He's called Mouse because he eats so much cheese. Mad for the stuff.'

Wilma's eyes widened. That sounded like a mountain-sized clue. She'd better write that down. She reached for her notebook and very quietly scribbled 'LOADS OF INK. CHEESY MAN' on a back page.

'He'll be getting deliveries organized now,' added Cicatrise, casting a glance at his fob watch. 'You'll have to hurry if you want to catch him. Why do you want to know about blue-cabbage bugs anyhow?'

'I'm afraid I'm not at liberty to say,' said Theodore, maintaining his guard. 'We're just investigating something that might affect the Ten-Annual Election.'

Cicatrise waved his hand dismissively. 'Bah! Ten-Annual

Election. Load of unnecessary bother. Anyway, I must be off. Things to do.' And with that he exited the kitchen just as a door behind them opened and in burst Brenda Blaize, grinning.

'Ho there!' she said, holding out her spare hand to shake Theodore's.

'Hello,' said Wilma, smiling. 'I'm an apprentice detective.'

Brenda smiled vaguely in her direction. 'Don't mind Hurl,' she went on in a slightly adoring tone. 'He's in a bit of a grump this morning. Must have had a late night. Usually he's a darling!'

Mr Goodman nodded slowly.

Must have been a VERY late night to be THAT rude, thought Wilma to herself.

'Anyway. Heard all about you from Glenda. Hope she's not running you ragged. She's a taskmaster and no mistake. Never get to see her properly. Ever been to the Strangely-shaped-vegetable Museum?'

'Er, not since I was a boy, no,' answered Theodore. 'I'd love to see it again. Though it would be useful to meet this Mouse chap first. Is he about? Farmer Hurl said he'd be getting your deliveries organized?'

'Actually, he's just fixing something for me. He should be finished soon. I'll take you to him,' beamed Brenda. 'His quarters are next to the museum. I can show you the strangely shaped vegetables while we wait for him. Oh, and grab that bucket,' she added, pointing to some peelings. 'We can feed the goat at the same time!'

The Strangely-shaped-vegetable Museum was homed in a stone outhouse, its door made entirely of carved wooden carrots. Brenda reached for a bunch of keys in her pocket. 'Oh!' she suddenly shouted, turning, 'Look out! Here comes the goat!'

Wilma spun round to see a large brown goat charging at speed towards Inspector Lemone, who was holding the bucket of peelings. Startled, he gave out a short squeal. Pickle, thinking this might be a situation in which he could try to be brave, quickly stood in front of Wilma to protect her and mustered a low, warning growl. But the goat, narrowing one eye, kicked out a back leg and sent Pickle flying without a second thought. Before anyone knew what was what, the goat gave Inspector Lemone a considerable butt, shoved Wilma out of the way with his rear end and descended on the bucket of peelings, which were then demolished in ten seconds flat.

'Told you he was bumpy,' said Brenda, with a shrug. 'Anyway, that's Mouse's quarters there.' She indicated a small outhouse. 'I'll just get the museum open.'

Wilma, who was dusting Pickle down after his tumble, suddenly spotted something out of the corner of her eye. Waiting until Brenda had gone inside, she bent down and picked up a small heap of torn pieces of paper. 'Look at this,' she said, whispering to Theodore and proffering the pieces. 'It's the Ten-Annual Election poster. The one everyone is meant to display. And it's all ripped up.'

Theodore's eyes narrowed in thought. 'Tuck those away in your pinafore pocket, Wilma. And well done for keeping it quiet. What top tip must we keep in mind at all times?'

'Number eight, Mr Goodman. Proper detectives always save what they're thinking till last.'

Theodore nodded and turned back towards the small outhouse next to the museum.

'Looks like he's not in,' said Lemone, who was knocking on Mouse's door.

Wilma came up behind him and peered in through the window. It all looked quite normal: large table with a plate of cheese on it, a few chairs, a fireplace with cold ash-tipped coals. But, in the corner of the room, Wilma spotted a smaller table with a dummy's head on it. The fake head had a thin strip of lace pinned to it, the corner of which was covered with a clump of hairs. 'What's that?' asked Wilma, pointing.

'A wig block,' explained Theodore, looking over her shoulder.

'Not in?' called out Brenda, suddenly poking her head round the carrot-carved door. 'My fault! I'm always getting him to do little things for me. Come on in then! I'll show you around the museum!'

The interior of the Strangely-shaped-vegetable Museum was brightly lit with large church-like windows allowing the morning sunshine to stream in. The room was filled with cabinets and wicker baskets and as they followed after Brenda Wilma noticed a large sign next to the desk at the entrance that read:

CHILDREN, ANIMALS AND LOWSIDERS
GO FREE!

Brenda was beaming.

'That's kind,' said Wilma, pointing to it.

Brenda nodded. 'Farmer Hurl's idea,' she said. 'He has quite firm views.' Brenda was clearly very proud of her museum, and brimming over with enthusiasm. 'Some of the strangely shaped vegetables in here are hundreds of years old,' she said eagerly. 'That's a mummified runner bean,' she added, pointing to a thin, dark object wrapped in a stained cloth. 'It's *ancient*. Haunted too, some say.'

Wilma peered in and gulped.

'Gosh, look at this!' exclaimed Lemone, pointing into another glass display case. 'This potato is shaped exactly like a . . . potato. Oh. Wait . . .'

'No,' explained Brenda. 'That's a *turnip* that's shaped like a potato. Amazing, isn't it? This is my favourite strangely shaped vegetable,' she added, leading them towards a rather grand podium. 'It's a courgette that looks like a cat sitting on a dog sitting on a woman knitting a cardigan.'

They all peered towards it.

'So it does,' nodded Lemone. 'If you squint. And turn your head sideways.'

'Anyway,' beamed Brenda, 'why do you want to know about blue cabbage?'

Theodore reached into his inside pocket and pulled out the Villains' Ball poster. Unfolding it, he began, 'These have been appearing all over the island. Confidentially, as you're the Cooperate General's sister, I can tell you that whoever made these has used a very distinctive ink. An ink, we now know, that is made from the widdybug, an insect that is only found in blue-cabbage patches. I'd quite like to take a look at the work shed if you could show us the way. I'm told Mouse makes the ink we're interested in. It would be helpful to take a proper look. Find out who's been using it. That sort of thing.'

'Oh,' answered Brenda, folding her arms, her smile fading a little. 'But there's lots more to see here. You've barely started the tour.'

Wilma had found herself in front of another display case in which pumpkins of various sizes were covered in all manner of moustaches, beards and hairpieces.

'Why are these pumpkins all hairy?' she asked, pointing towards them.

Brenda, looking a little distracted, glanced over. 'Oh, Mouse makes me wigs and things from the goat hair. We sometimes put plays on here at the museum. I get everyone to take a part. Mouse, Cicatrise, the goat. It's silly! We had a box of them. So we dressed up the pumpkins for fun.'

Wilma stared back into the display case. One pumpkin's moustache was missing. Her eyes widened. Was it ANOTHER clue? She glanced over her shoulder towards Theodore, caught his eye and surreptitiously pointed towards the bare-faced pumpkin. Clearing his throat, Theodore turned back to Brenda. 'So the work shed? You said you'd show us the way?'

The work shed was behind the farmhouse, up a muddy track just north of the meadow.

'Aren't the butterbuds lovely?' said Brenda, pointing to a scattering of yellow flowers climbing up an old stone wall. 'It's such a shame they smell of sour milk. Quite revolting close up. Oh, look,' she added, pointing up into the sky, 'a bizzclaw! Think we've got a breeding pair. That's exciting, isn't it?'

Wilma looked up and watched as the large, brightly coloured bird circled above them.

Brenda Blaize, thought Wilma, was quite like her headmistress, Kite Lambard – perfectly lovely but a bit of a higgledy-piggledy-brain. Neither of them could concentrate for a single second. Perhaps this was what Glenda Blaize had meant when she'd described her sister as 'highly strung'.

'What task is Mouse doing for you?' asked Theodore, as they walked.

'Fixing a chimney pot,' replied Brenda.

Wilma shifted her gaze back towards the house and looked up towards the roof. A young man was staring back at her. Her eyes widened.

'I couldn't fix a chimney pot myself,' muttered Inspector Lemone, picking a blackberry from a bush and popping it in his mouth. 'I hate heights.'

'He doesn't mind a bit,' replied Brenda, leading them on. 'That boy's like a mountain goat.'

Wilma's eyes widened again. There was someone else she'd seen recently who was very good at climbing. She gave a little gasp, then bit her bottom lip quickly so as not to give her excitement away. Could this be FOUR massive clues in the space of five minutes?

'Well, here's the work shed. And that's where we get the widdybugs from,' exclaimed Brenda, pointing towards a long rectangle of turned-over earth just next to the blue-cabbage patch. 'Pass me that spade would you?'

Wilma looked behind her and saw a stack of gardening tools hanging from hooks on a wooden fence. Taking the spade, she passed it over.

Brenda grinned. 'Hope you don't mind creepy crawlies!' she laughed. 'Widdybugs are a bit gruesome!'

Wilma gave a small smile back. To be honest, she wasn't that interested in the widdybugs any more, and kept looking over her shoulder towards the house and that young man up by the chimney pot. The widdybug ink, the torn-up poster outside his house, the moustaches, the climbing! He had to be the one they were after! Wilma turned back and tried to catch Mr Goodman's attention without giving the game away.

Brenda struck the spade down into the earth and thrust her foot against its top edge so the blade went ever deeper.

'So you were saying Mouse makes the ink,' said Theodore, his moustache giving a little twitch. 'In what quantities?'

'We get about ten big bottles out of them a year,' replied Brenda, digging down. 'Mind you, it is an unusual colour. So we don't sell many. I think the last one we sold was a few months back. Can't remember who to. You'll have to check the delivery records. Ah ha! Here we go! A cluster of them. Look at that, Mr Goodman! Widdybugs!'

Theodore bent down and, reaching into the hole, pulled up a handful of thick creamy-coloured bugs. 'Ugly things, aren't they?' he said, getting out his magnifying glass to take a look. 'Come here, Wilma. Have a look at them through this.' He stopped and stared at his apprentice, who, in a state of some agitation, had been standing behind Brenda Blaize, pulling faces for all she was worth. She could still see Mouse on the roof. This was maddening!

Brenda looked at her watch. 'Are you going to be much longer? It's just the museum . . .' Her voice trailed off and she stared into the distance.

Wilma continued staring hard at Mr Goodman. Perhaps she could whisper something into his ear when Brenda was being especially distracted? Yes. She'd try that. So Wilma strode over to take a closer look at the widdybugs.

Wilma had never been allowed to touch Mr Goodman's magnifying glass before. It was a great honour. It was a lot heavier than she had thought it would be and the leather round the golden handle was soft and silky to the touch. It would be a long time until she was given her own detective's magnifying glass, of course. You don't get one until you've graduated from the Academy. But, one day, Wilma hoped she'd have a magnifying glass just like Mr Goodman's.

Wilma quickly glanced back up at the roof. Mouse was still there. Somehow she HAD to tell Mr Goodman. Wilma leaned towards Theodore's ear and whispered, 'Roooooof.'

'Sorry,' said Brenda, looking quickly at Wilma. 'What was that?'

'Ruff, ruff,' explained Wilma, trying to cover her tracks. 'I was talking to Pickle. Oh, bleeuuuuuurgh!' she yelled, changing the subject quickly. 'These widdybugs are the most horrible things I've ever seen. They've got legs coming out of their faces! And fangs! And really bad haircuts.'

Wilma raised her head from the magnifying glass and looked up towards the rooftop once more. Mouse was gone! This was highly unsatisfactory.

'You mentioned delivery records?' pressed Theodore, glancing at his watch. 'Can I see them?'

Brenda nodded. 'They'll be in the work shed.'

Wilma desperately wanted to speak to Theodore about Mouse. She was quite convinced that he might be a proper suspect, but she had to stick to top tip number eight. She'd just have to wait. It was KILLING her. .

*

The work shed was a maelstrom of mess. Heaps of papers, boxes, old tools that needed fixing, buckets, piles of string, seedling trays, compost bags and a juicing machine next to which sat a half-full jar of dead widdybugs. Everywhere Wilma looked, it was chaos.

'Right,' said Brenda, clapping her hands together optimistically, 'the delivery book should be in here somewhere. Not quite sure where. Oh! *There's* that hammer. Been looking for that for days.'

'Delivery book?' said Cicatrise Hurl, suddenly appearing out of nowhere behind them. 'I lost it, remember? I dropped it down the well by accident.'

'Oh yes,' said Brenda, frowning. 'That's a bother. I suppose we could try to dredge the well. Might take days though. And the book's probably unreadable now.'

Theodore's moustache twitched slightly. 'Brenda here says you had a late night. Anything exciting?'

'Not really, no,' shrugged the farmer. Everyone waited for him to elaborate, but it quickly became clear he had nothing further to say on the matter.

'Nice map of Cooper,' said Lemone, who was peering up at a rather ornate display on the work-shed wall.

'Delivery route,' explained Cicatrise, leaning past him to pick up a trowel from the long trestle table. 'Excuse me. Need this.'

Wilma looked up at the map. It was covered in dots. Dots, Wilma noticed, that were in lots of the same places as the dots for the targets she'd pinned on her Clue Board! She gave another squeak. Five clues. FIVE!

'That's funny,' said Brenda, looking around the work shed. 'Could have sworn I had a box of those inks in here. Looks like it's gone. Was going to give you a bottle.'

Theodore, Wilma noticed, was *still* not looking at her. This was EXASPERATING. Instead, he seemed to be sniffing the air.

'Quite a distinct smell in here, Miss Blaize,' he said. 'Could you tell me what it is?'

'That sweet smell? Might be the boiled mumblebugs. We've been making them to sell at the election ceremonies.'

Wilma sniffed the air too. There was something recognizable about that aroma, but she couldn't put her finger on it . . .

'Will that be all?' asked Brenda, with some urgency. 'I really do need to be getting on. Mouse'll be around shortly, I'm sure.'

'Thank you, Miss Blaize. By all means. Don't let us keep you. And don't worry. We're fine waiting.'

As Brenda strode off through the door, the smile on Theodore's face fell. Checking that they were alone, he turned to Wilma and the inspector with some urgency.

'Lactose!' he declared. 'That's the smell I was struggling to identify when the smoke bombs went off. Lactose is a vital ingredient in smoke bombs! Write that down, Wilma!'

'Mr Goodman!' Wilma cried out, jumping up and down. 'That makes it six clues! SIX! The missing moustache, the ink, the torn-up poster, the map on the wall with all the dots that are in the same places as my dots on my Clue Board, the lactose thing and I saw him! I saw the Mouse man jumping around on the roof. It's SO obvious. He *must* be the Masked Man!' And with that, she heaved a huge sigh of relief.

'It might not be that obvious, Wilma,' said Theodore, deep in thought. 'In fact, it's almost too obvious. Farmer Hurl was being highly evasive and odd too. All the same, the quicker we speak to him the better.'

Lemone, hearing hoofs, ran suddenly to the door. 'Oh no,' he called back. 'Someone's dashed off on horseback! Now what?'

'He's trying to escape!' yelled Wilma frantically. 'Only guilty people do that, Mr Goodman!'

'To the tandem!' cried Theodore, running out of the shed, Lemone, Wilma and Pickle in tow. 'Cooper may depend on it!'

'Perhaps,' panted Wilma, 'if we can't find Mouse, we could set a trap? I've got some cheese in my pinafore pocket. We could use it as a lure.'

'I don't think his love of cheese is going to help us, Wilma,' replied Theodore, leaping astride the tandem. 'Bother! Mouse has already disappeared from view.'

Inspector Lemone took out his watch and glanced at it. 'Oh no! The Placing of the Names Ceremony starts in two hours!'

'Then let's head to the Central Plaza,' cried Theodore, pressing down hard on the pedals. 'We can position ourselves at vantage points. If the Masked Man, or Mouse, turns up, we'll be ready for them.'

Inspector Lemone cast a glance over his shoulder towards Wilma and Pickle in the trailer. 'I'll take that cheese, if it's going spare?'

Wilma took the cheese from her pocket and blew some fluff off it before handing it to Inspector Lemone.

'Ugh. Bit claggy,' he mumbled, grimacing a little as he bit into it. 'How long has it been in your pocket?'

Wilma pursed her lips and started counting on her fingers. 'About three months.'

Never mind the cheese! There's a chase afoot! Oh, quickly! QUICKLY!

134

Chapter 15

'**W**hat do you think?' said Barbu, holding up two waistcoats. 'Red or purple? I like the red because it says bold and dynamic, but then the purple says, "Hello! I'm fun at weekends!" I can't choose.'

'Perhaps you should wear this one, master,' suggested Janty, picking out a jet-black waistcoat from a pile on a chair. 'It says, "I'm evil and I'm not remotely worried about my height."'

Barbu shot his apprentice a livid stare and, snatching the waistcoat, barked, 'All the evil greats were reduced in stature. That's historical FACT. And, besides, I am not short. Even if I may appear to be. It's an optical illusion.'

Janty stared back and said nothing.

'But I *will* wear this black waistcoat. NOT because of the height thing. But because it matches my eyes.' Janty raised an

135

eyebrow. 'I mean my soul. Obviously,' added Barbu quickly. 'My evil, evil soul.'

Janty, who was standing next to the window with his arms folded, sighed and looked out. When he'd agreed to be Barbu's evil apprentice, it had been in the wake of his father, Visser Haanstra, dying. Recently he'd found himself wondering whether this was the life that his father would have wanted for him. Yes, Visser had been a master forger and used his skill for criminal gain, but being born on the Lowside hadn't given him many other options. If Visser had been born on the Farside, his talents would have been lauded as great art. Janty had the same gift as his father. And perhaps it wasn't too late for him. Perhaps Wilma was right. There was another way.

'My frockcoat, Janty,' shouted Barbu from across the room.

Another way that did not mean being skivvy to a short, moody maniac who didn't appreciate his abilities.

But before Janty could do as he was told a face appeared at the windowpane, making Janty jump. There, hanging upside down and waving, was the Masked Man. 'Can you let me in?' he mouthed. 'I'm dangling from a drainpipe!'

'Oh God, he's here, he's HERE,' squealed Barbu, dashing for the frockcoat and checking his hair quickly in the mirror.

'Thanks,' panted the Masked Man, as Janty helped him into the room. 'Thought I'd come *over* rather than *up through* the

Twelve Rats' Tails. Can't be too careful. Everywhere I go I'm being chased. Well! Hello again! Nice waistcoat!'

Barbu's eyes brightened. 'Thank you. Tailored, of course. I get them from Stitch and Darn on Buttons Row. Do you use them?'

The Masked Man shook his head.

'Oh they're very good,' continued Barbu, unbuttoning his waistcoat. 'Look at that lining. It's made of *fur*. Would you like to stroke it?'

'No, thanks.'

'Right, of course!' said Barbu, briskly. 'To business! Janty, fetch up some squifty juice for our guest and don't you have those plans to be getting on with?'

'Oh no, no squifty juice for me, thanks!' smiled the Masked Man, taking a seat and crossing his legs. 'I never drink and connive.'

'Probably for the best,' nodded Barbu, pacing nervously and shooing Janty from the room. 'So. Evil! Let's talk evil! What's the plan? What do you *need*?'

'I'm not really sure. I suppose I came up with the notion that if we could somehow extricate the riches of the Farside during the Final Naming Ceremony then perhaps the Lowside wouldn't be so downtrodden in the future. But then I don't really want anyone to be robbed. Well. I say that, but perhaps we could rob

137

them but then give everything back? Like a lesson learned? That sort of thing? And I certainly don't want anyone to be hurt.'

Barbu blinked. This was a conundrum. Here he was with a visionary, of that there was no doubt, but a visionary who had no practical understanding of how being evil actually worked.

'Riiiiiight,' he began, biting his bottom lip. 'The thing is, Masked . . . You don't mind if I call you Masked?'

'By all means . . .'

'I suspect, given that you're a little *green* around the edges when it comes to foul play, that you should probably take a back seat in all this. Let's stick to my suggestion. *You* be the ideas man and *I'll* take care of the rest.'

'You won't harm anyone though, will you?' asked the Masked Man, leaning forward.

Barbu hesitated for a moment and pressed his fingers together as if in prayer. 'Well . . .' he began, giving a little shrug, 'if I said *not much*, would that be acceptable?'

The Masked Man frowned, deep in thought. 'And it'll mean the Lowside isn't put upon any more? And things are fairer?'

'Oh YES,' insisted Barbu, mustering an expression of intense sincerity. 'I can guarantee that as far as *I'm* concerned, things will be *vastly* fairer.'

The Masked Man grinned. 'All right then,' he said, standing

and holding out his hand. 'We have a deal.'

As they shook on it, Tully, carrying several large packets over his shoulder, bundled in through the door. 'Got the assembly kit, master,' he said, throwing them all into a heap on the floor.

'Assembly kit?' asked the Masked Man, smiling. 'What's that for?'

Barbu, his eyes flashing momentarily with panic, blustered forward. 'Oh, nothing! Just a couple of cupboards! The decor here is so . . . bare,' he said, gesturing at the already furniture-stuffed room. 'I think living quarters should have that cramped feel. Don't you? It's very *now*.'

'Oh,' said the stupid henchman, 'was I supposed to get cupboards? I thought I was getting—'

'Yes, yes,' snapped Barbu quickly, throwing a dressing gown over Tully's face. 'Sleep now, gentle giant! Well! I think we all know what we're doing. Lovely to see you again, Masked! And any questions . . . you know where I am!' And with some haste he steered the well-meaning crusader back over to the open window. 'Goodbye! Bye-bye!'

He waved as the Masked Man climbed out and disappeared back over the roof.

'God, Tully!' Barbu yelled, as soon as the coast was clear. 'Could you be any more idiotic?'

'Sorry, master,' said Tully, from under the dressing gown. 'Shall I sleep now? Like you told me to?'

'No of course not, you reeking fool!' screamed the diminutive villain. 'Start assembling that cow. We haven't got much time left!'

Sorry? Did he just say *cow*?

Chapter 16

The Placing of the Names Ceremony was the second official observance in the Ten-Annual Election. During it, Glenda Blaize would place every eligible name into the Grand Tombola and then, to celebrate, there would be another glorious parade. The plaza, like yesterday, was rammed to bursting and Glenda had taken her place up on the podium, with Dromley fussing behind her. To her left Melba Toest, Kite, Captain Brock and the 2nd Hawks Brigade were keeping a watchful eye on things.

The Grand Tombola was hidden behind a set of plush red curtains. Dromley crept to the back of the podium and carried a thick velvet cord towards Glenda, who then pulled it. The curtains parted, and across the Central Plaza wild cheers rang out as the tombola once again came into view. Wilma and Pickle had positioned themselves on the bottom ledge of a lamp post and were scanning the square and the rooftops, but there was no sign of the Masked Man, or Mouse.

'Citizens of Cooper!' called out Glenda Blaize, and silence quickly descended upon the eager crowd. 'The time has come to commence the practicalities of the Ten-Annual Election. In this golden sack, I have the names of every eligible Farsider. The names shall be placed into the tombola, which will be turned by the Wooden Hand of Coop for twenty-four hours. We will meet here again tomorrow, for the Final Naming Ceremony!'

Another cheer went up from the crowd. Glenda held a shimmering cotton bag upward. It was bulging, stuffed with small paper slips.

Wilma stared at her mentor, who was standing nearer the stage. She thought again about the election process and felt a funny knot in her stomach. He was the noblest, finest man she knew. How Theodore P. Goodman's name could not be allowed to be in the Ten-Annual Election was beyond her. No wonder Lowsiders were disgruntled. All the same, it wasn't right to try to change things by stealing and making mischief. Wilma was a Lowsider too and, like her hero, she was going to dedicate her life to doing the right thing, and hopefully, one day, she would be as respected as Mr Goodman.

'And now, in keeping with tradition,' called out Melba Toest, Keeper of Cooper Law, who was reading from an official document, 'the Cooperate General shall draw one name from the golden sack! And that first Farsider shall be the first into the tombola and honoured by receiving the Ceremonial Duck.'

'Hold it up, Dromley,' added Glenda, looking over her shoulder.

Behind her, Dromley Abbams was struggling to pick up a small but noisy bird. He had managed to get his hands about its middle, but every time the duck flapped its wings Dromley, who had the strength of a damp rag, screamed like a little girl.

Glenda rolled her eyes. 'Put it back in the crate, Dromley,' she barked. 'Honestly, I knew I shouldn't have let you do anything important.'

Kite, seeing that Dromley was struggling, went over to help. 'I'll take the duck, Mr Abbams,' she said, tucking the bird expertly under her armpit. 'The trick is pinning down the wings.'

Wilma raised her eyebrows. Well, well, Miss Lambard *was* good at something.

'And now,' continued Melba, 'let us learn who is to be the first Farsider name into the tombola and the recipient of the Ceremonial Duck!'

People craned for a better view and children were being lifted on to their parent's shoulders so they could see too.

Glenda plunged her arm into the golden sack. The tension in the square was palpable.

'And the first Farsider is . . .' cried Glenda, pulling out a slip of paper and unfolding it, 'Boiled Hyltton!'

One small scream went up from the left of the plaza and Wilma could just see a bald man in spectacles jumping up and down for joy.

'That's me!' he was yelling. 'Me!'

A polite ripple of applause broke out across the square as the jubilant Farsider pushed his way towards the stage.

'And so, Boiled Hyltton,' said Melba, gesturing towards Kite, 'here is the Ceremonial Duck. As you know, you must not eat it, but must now carry it with you at all times in keeping with Cooper Law.'

'Oh,' said Boiled, his smile fading. 'I'd sort of forgotten about that bit.'

'May you and your duck be very happy together,' added Glenda, gesturing to a bugler to her right who played a short, triumphant fanfare. 'And now . . .' said Glenda, taking Boiled Hyltton's name and placing it in the Grand Tombola, 'the rest of the names shall go into the tombola. Dromley! Close the curtains! Sound the fanfare! Let the parade commence!'

Horns blasted a glorious salute as the names were tipped inside the tombola and the Wooden Hand of Coop began to slowly turn it. The thick red curtains drew closed once more, not to open again till the ceremonial draw the next day. Wilma could see the parade of floats arriving at the far end of the Central Plaza. At the front was a magnificently decorated giant shoe crammed full of people dressed like socks. Behind that there was a dazzling display from the Cooper Trampolineteers, the crowd cheering wildly every time one of them bounced upward. Then behind that, Wilma noticed, was a float that didn't quite have the pizzazz of the others.

It was in the shape of a badly constructed cow. The horns were skew-whiff, the eyes were uneven and it was wearing a floor-length floral skirt that looked for all the world like a shower curtain that had been ripped down and wrapped round it at a moment's notice. Wilma's eyes narrowed. There were three people with this float, all dressed as milk churns, two walking either side of the cow and a third very small milk churn sitting astride it and waving. Wilma felt the stirrings of a Hunchy Instinct, that strange, familiar feeling that could be mistaken for indigestion but which actually meant, in her experience as an apprentice detective, that fishy shenanigans were afoot. Something about that float wasn't right. She needed a closer look.

'Come on, Pickle,' said Wilma, jumping off the ledge. 'Let's try to squeeze a bit nearer the front.'

Pushing gently through the cheering crowds, Wilma soon found herself just in front of the main stage. The cow had come to an abrupt halt and people on the floats behind it were shouting at the milk churn on top of the cow to get moving. He, in turn, was holding out his arms as if there was nothing to be done. The cow was going nowhere.

And where were the other two milk churns? thought Wilma. Then suddenly, from behind the cow, the other churns reappeared. The smaller of the two made a thumbs-up gesture to the one on top and, the cow started up again, much to everyone's relief. Wilma's Hunchy Instinct grew stronger.

'Mr Goodman,' she called, pushing her way back to where she'd spotted the great detective, 'I think something might not be right. That float, the cow one, is rubbish. Why would there be a rubbishy float in the greatest parade in ten years? All the other floats are properly amazing. But that one looks as if it's been knocked together by a short-sighted monkey. And why would a rubbishy float then get stuck at the front of the main stage, right by the red curtains that are guarding the Grand Tombola?' Wilma put a hand to her mouth and gave a fulsome burp. 'I knew it. It *is* a hunch! I always get wind when I have a hunch.'

Theodore stared after the ramshackle display and frowned. 'Interesting observation, Wilma. I think we should investigate. Somehow we need to check behind those curtains and make sure the tombola is OK without causing a drama!'

'I could crawl under them, if you like, Mr Goodman,' offered Wilma. 'I'm small enough to slip under unnoticed.'

'Good thinking,' answered Theodore, with a nod. 'You do that, I'll alert the others and we'll all meet at the front to the left of the stage. Tread carefully, Wilma.'

Wilma was thrilled. Here she was, being trusted with massive tasks. She didn't quite know what she was looking for, but she felt that if there was anything wrong then she'd surely spot it.

Making her way over to the other side of the stage, where she was protected from view by a cluster of small trees, she pulled herself quickly up on to the platform and, a second later, she was under the curtain and out of sight. It was quite dark on the other side of the curtain; the thick, red velvet effectively blocked out the light. As her eyes adjusted, Wilma could see the Grand Tombola being turned by the Wooden Hand of Coop and there was a rich smell of shaved wood and polish.

The Grand Tombola was an object of great beauty. It was made from intricately carved wood and painted with gold leaf. She walked over to it and inspected it closely. The carvings seemed to be of small tableaux, no doubt taken from ancient Cooper history. There was the story of the Brackle Bush – one that every child on Cooper knew – and the Bear of Mithering that once got loose and ran amok on the trout farm, and another tableau, smaller than the others, of a small boy standing with a taller man. Must be a father and son, thought Wilma. She didn't know this story. Oh well. As far as she could tell, nothing was out of order. Perhaps her hunch was indigestion, after all. She'd had three wet cakes so it wasn't impossible. All the same, it was going to be mildly embarrassing telling Mr Goodman that everything was fine when she'd made such a fuss.

'Well,' said Theodore, who was waiting at the side of the stage when she emerged, 'what did you discover?'

Wilma shook her head. 'Nothing I'm afraid, Mr Goodman,' she said, her cheeks reddening. 'Though I did discover the tombola is beautifully carved with images from Cooper's history – though there was one about a father and son that I didn't recognize . . .' she trailed off. 'Sorry. I made a right fuss about that cow and for no reason, it seems.'

Theodore put a reassuring hand on her shoulder. 'It's good that you're paying attention to your instincts, Wilma. They're all a detective really has in the end.'

Wilma smiled gratefully, though she still felt a bit disappointed.

Theodore turned to the group and addressed them in a sombre tone. 'So there it is. We now have twenty-four hours to either find the Masked Man and stop him from mobilizing all the Criminal Elements of the Lowside against us, or . . .'

'Or what, Goodman?' asked Inspector Lemone, tensely wiping his brow.

'Or drastic preventative measures may have to be taken,' answered Theodore, in the gravest of tones. 'I'm afraid there is only one other possible course of action left to us. To the offices of the Cooperate General! We must seek the approval of our leader in her last day of office. And it'll be the gravest decision of her life!'

What course of action? WHAT COURSE OF ACTION? AND WHAT GRAVE DECISION? Oh! I can hardly BEAR IT!

Chapter 17

'So what you're telling me,' began Glenda Blaize, 'is that we're looking at potential multiple robberies of multiple locations all over the island tomorrow during the Naming Ceremony and we have no idea who is behind it or how to stop them?'

'I'm afraid that's right, Madam Cooperate,' nodded Theodore. 'And if we can't prevent him, by either reason or force, then we simply don't have sufficient manpower to protect every possible target.'

Captain Brock looked grave. 'Perhaps I should have my men out seeing if they get wind of any mass meetings?'

'I think it's too late for that, Captain,' said Theodore regretfully. 'We should certainly carry on looking for Mouse. It's imperative that I question him. He may be the Masked Man, he may not, but I have no doubt that he's the key to unravelling this mess. But I'm afraid our main priority now must be to protect the property and the people of the Farside by any means necessary. We're completely outnumbered and if the Criminal Elements all strike at once we could be in very grave danger. Lowsiders good and bad too. Imagine what might follow . . . riots, recriminations, chaos . . . And there's only one way I can think of stopping Lowsiders entering the Farside.'

possibly one looked at each other nervously. What could he

Theodore sighed heavily. It's only happened once before in the whole of Cooper history, during the Great Revolt, but I fear it must happen again. The gate in the Great Wall must be closed!'

Wilma gasped, her eyes as large as saucers. The border gate between the Farside and the Lowside was to be shut and bolted. This was as serious a matter as she could ever imagine. A dread silence filled the room.

Then Glenda spoke.

'Is this doable, Melba?'

The bookish law keeper blinked, gulped and nodded. 'In extreme circumstances, yes. A Cooperate General can give the order.'

'It seems we have no choice,' declared Glenda gravely. 'Dromley, let it be known that I *am* giving the order. To the Great Wall! There's not a moment to lose!'

151

'But . . .' called out Wilma, running after everyone as they hurried from the room, 'it will be opened again, won't it? Won't it?'

Nobody answered her. Because nobody had the answer.

The scene at the Great Wall was one of shock and pandemonium. Never before in living memory had the border gat___ __g barricaded shut and people on both sid_ much love lost in stunned silence. There had between Farsiders and Lowsiders, but, all the same, it was still upsetting.

Crowds of angry Lowsiders were being marshalled along the rim of the wall and back through the Great Gate while the Farsiders looked on in confusion. Dark clouds were gathering to the east and a metallic-smelling wind was picking up pace, a sure sign that more rain was on its way. Wilma hooked her billowing plaits behind her ears and bent down to give Pickle a reassuring stroke. She didn't know what to feel. She understood that this was their only option if a mass robbery was to be avoided, but as she watched the 2nd Hawks Brigade heaving the Great Gate shut she felt a sharp tug inside her.

She looked up at Mr Goodman. She had never seen the great detective look more serious than now. To his right stood Glenda, grave-faced and frowning.

'We must make it quite clear,' said Glenda, deep in thought, 'that this is a necessity. Not all Lowsiders are untrustworthy, of course they're not. It is because of the Criminal Elements who seek to control this island that good people must suffer, but it's our only option, however regrettable.'

Suddenly, to their left, Wilma saw Cicatrise Hurl striding towards them, Brenda running after him.

'What's the meaning of this?' he called out, his face set with frowns. 'It's a disgrace!'

'Glenda!' begged Brenda, her eyes filling up. 'I implore you! Don't do this!'

'I'm sorry,' said Glenda, steely with resolve. 'The island is in peril. It's my job to protect it.'

'It's your job to protect everybody!' replied Cicatrise, his eyes aflame. 'And that includes the Lowsiders! Not all of them are bad, but you're leaving them to the mercy of the Criminal Elements.'

Brenda stared up at Cicatrise and nodded, her tears now falling thick and fast. 'This is awful,' she mumbled. 'I never thought this would happen. Never.'

'None of us did,' sighed Glenda, taking a cigar out from her top breast pocket and chewing on it. 'And I am sorry for it.'

'It's our only option, Mr Hurl,' said Theodore, stepping in to diffuse the situation. 'If you want to be of help, you can tell me

153

if you have any idea where your yard lad, Mouse, is. I must speak with him urgently.'

Cicatrise, who was still livid, shook his head. 'No. I don't. There are slightly more important things on my mind.'

Brenda, who was still gazing at him, nodded in agreement.

Over by the wall Wilma could see Trevor, who looked inconsolable. His face was upturned, his mouth set in a desolate howl. He was being held up by another man with wild ginger hair and a woman who had the biggest front teeth Wilma had ever seen.

'NOT THE GAAAAAAATE!' wailed Trevor, snot pouring from his nose. 'NOT THE GAAAAAAAAAAAAAAAAAAAATE! Oh, Susan! This is the worst day of my LIIIIIIIIIIFE! And I couldn't find the paperwork! I looked in the rules. There's a form that needs filling in when the Gate is closed. I COULDN'T FIND IIIIIIIIIT! UH HUH HUH HUH HUH HUH!'

The woman with the enormous teeth shot a helpless look in the direction of her ginger-haired companion, who was now trying to wipe Trevor's nose with the end of his tie.

'Dry your eyes,' she said, giving him a pat on the shoulder. 'We can use the emergency form.'

'Emergency form?' gulped Trevor, rubbing his eyes with the back of his hand.

'I've got one here,' she said, poking two fingers into a tiny pocket at the end of her shirt collar. 'In case of emergencies! And here we are! In an emergency!' With some difficulty she pulled out a tiny slip of red folded paper, which, when unfolded, was about the size of a stamp. 'We all need to sign this. Three times. And then we're covered. Did anyone bring a pen?' Silence fell across them. 'Oh,' said Susan, a little crestfallen.

'UH HUH HUH HUH HUH HUH HUH!' wailed Trevor, again.

Wilma looked up to the top rim of the wall where mouldy vegetables were being thrown over by the Lowsiders in the direction of Inspector Lemone, who was dragging a large wooden pole towards the now almost closed gate. He was covered in tomato pips and dirty potato peelings and was a vision of abject misery. Theodore shook his head. Things were in danger of getting out of hand.

An ominous low boom drew everyone's attention as the Great Gate finally swung shut. Lemone and a few of the men from the 2nd Hawks Brigade then stoically lifted the wooden bar into place. The gate could not now be opened from the Lowside.

A chorus of angry cries and whistles carried over from the other side of the wall while the Farsiders stood in near silence.

Glenda, realizing that everyone had turned to look at her, cleared her throat. 'Citizens of Cooper, a dark day has fallen on this island! For reasons it is felt safer not to go into, those in charge believe this action is in the best interests of everyone. But I promise you that as soon as the Final Naming Ceremony is completed, I shall give the order for the gate to be reopened!'

'But you won't be in charge!' yelled Cicatrise, his eyes blazing. 'How do we know the new Cooperate General will open it up again?'

There was a dissatisfied rumble from the crowd.

Glenda held up her hand for quiet. 'You are quite right. I shall no longer be in charge. But let us hope that whoever is drawn from the tombola tomorrow will take counsel from me and do the decent thing.'

Theodore, looking out into the crowd, sensed the unrest. Leaning in towards Glenda, he took her by the elbow. 'Madam Cooperate,' he whispered, 'I think it's best we escort you back to the parliament building. Brock! Lemone!' he called. 'Lead the way! Wilma, Pickle, we'll take the rear.'

As they walked away from the Great Gate, Wilma tucked in behind Theodore and kept close to his heel. She'd never seen the Farsiders so agitated and then it struck her – perhaps they weren't cross with the Lowsiders . . . Perhaps they were cross that the island had been divided. And if that was true then that could only be a good thing.

'There's always hope,' she whispered to herself, thinking once again about Max and Pru and whether or not they would ever find them.

'Now what?' yelled a thick-necked man, staring up at the Great Gate from the Lowside once the more innocent Lowsiders had dissipated sadly. 'How are we supposed to pull off the biggest robbery of the century when we can't even get into the place we're supposed to rob?'

'And where's the Masked Man?' yelled a one-eyed man with teeth like gravestones.

Janty shrugged. 'Perhaps he's stuck on the Farside.'

'How dare you doubt him! If I want your useless opinion,' sneered Barbu, 'then I shall ask for it. Tully, pass me that barrel and then help me on to it. I shall speak to the rabble.'

Tully rolled an old squifty-juice barrel into place and then, as ordered, picked Barbu up like an evil baby and tossed him on top of it.

'Scum! Scoundrels! Villains!' Barbu began, tossing his magnificent quiff into a peak. 'The time has come for us to put into action the plans that the Masked Man has laid before us! Unfortunately, he can't be with us. But he entrusted his plan to me! And it's changed slightly. So. Here it is. Firstly, everywhere on the Farside is to be robbed at the same time! Janty – the map! Now organize yourselves into evil squadrons. Quickly! We haven't got all day!'

Barbu and his cohorts spent the next hour outlining exactly how each robbery would happen, what insider know-how was needed and, most importantly, how it would all end.

'But we still can't get through the gate to the Farside in the first place!' called a voice at the back as Barbu's lecture came to a close.

Barbu gritted his teeth. 'Tully,' he muttered, leaning down, 'when I'm finished, find that man and kill him.'

'Yes, master,' replied the stupid henchman.

'Yes, I know we still can't get through the gate,' snapped Barbu. 'And that is why we are going to go *underground*. Not many people know this, but there's a series of intricate and comprehensive tunnels into the Farside that run directly from underneath Rascal Rock.'

'But we can't get in there,' called the voice again. 'It's been seized.'

Barbu leaned down towards Tully again. 'When you kill him, Tully,' he spat, 'kill him really horribly.'

'Yes, master.'

'You are right again and that is why I am now declaring myself the Leader of the Lowside Criminal Elements and announcing that we, the dirtiest rogues on the island, are going to take back what's mine. We are going to liberate Rascal Rock!'

A great cheer went up and Barbu, elated with the way things were going and loving the attention, thrust his cane skyward.

'REVENGE SHALL BE MINE!' he cried, as, overhead, thunder ripped the sky and the heavens opened.

Oh dear. There's not a single positive to take from this. So let's all move swiftly on.

Chapter 18

Gerald Mothma didn't get paid much. He had been employed by the Cooper Office for People Who Owe Loads as a Seized Property Monitor for the past two years and was yet to be promoted. Physically, he was of average build and possessed a sweet face with lashes far longer than a young man deserved. He had led a quiet and unassuming life and lived alone in a small cottage in That Place Under There. He liked to hum as he walked and sometimes, when no one was listening, he derived great joy from burping. His only excitement was when, once a week, a young lady called Jenyfer Heel delivered his cheese. She had bright blue eyes and a head of golden curls, and every time Gerald saw her he felt a little lost.

In short, Gerald Mothma had never found himself in any sort of bother. He was a gentle soul. He had no idea whether he was brave, simply because he had never had occasion to be so. But

Gerald Mothma's day of reckoning was upon him. And he knew nothing about it.

The skies above Rascal Rock were dark and heavy and, as the rain lashed down, Gerald Mothma pulled the hood of his waxy oilskin overcoat a little further over his head. Behind him, the four security administrators were huddling under a makeshift tarpaulin, attempting to dry out their notebooks.

Thunder rumbled ominously to the west and Gerald looked up as a flash of sheet lightning briefly illuminated the gloom. Dusk had fallen quickly and a thick fog now rolled in from the sea. Somewhere out on the waves the low horn of a ship moaned. It was cold. Gerald tied his scarf a little tighter. In an hour he might have some soup and a good lump of the cheese Jenyfer Heel had brought him that morning. Perhaps next week, when she came again, he might try talking to her and say more than 'hello' and 'thank you'. Yes, he thought to himself. This time he definitely would.

Something moved in his peripheral vision. Something large and indefinable. Gerald looked towards the path that led away from Rascal Rock, but the thick blanket of fog obscured his view. Another grumble of thunder sounded overhead, a little closer and louder this time.

Probably just tricks of the night, thought Gerald, wiping the rain from the end of his nose.

A gust of wind howled over the cliff top, sending ripples through the fog as if a large stone had been dropped in water. A window of clear air appeared briefly, and there it was again – movement coming from the top of the pathway. Gerald frowned and reached for the lantern that hung by his side.

'Hey there,' he called to the security administrators, 'did you just see that?' He gestured up the pathway. 'Thought I saw something move.'

The security administrators all turned as one, peering into the darkness, then looked back at Gerald and shook their heads. Another lightning bolt flared across the sky and the fog, thick and impenetrable in the dark, was momentarily transparent. Gerald's eyes widened, his mouth fell open. There *was* something coming down the path and it was *massive*.

'What *is* that?' he mumbled to himself, straining to see as the thick gloom set in once more.

Suddenly a small rock struck the ground beside him. He looked down and frowned. Then another landed, then a third hit him on the arm.

'Ow!' he yelled out. He glanced quickly back towards the security administrators. Rocks were flying out of the fog and the four of them ducked and dived to avoid being hit.

'We're under attack,' whispered Gerald, blinking rapidly.

162

'Goodness gracious. This has never happened before. What are we going to do?'

From the fog loomed the small army of Criminal Elements. All were carrying weapons, all were snarling and scowling. At their helm was Barbu D'Anvers, who Gerald recognized instantly.

'Oh no,' Gerald gulped. 'Oh no. Not him. He's come to take back Rascal Rock. I can't let that happen!'

It was at this moment that Gerald Mothma, once a man of meek sensibilities who had never thought to raise a fist in his life, realized that if he was going to do his duty he needed to dig deep and find some courage. The Cooper Office for People Who Owe Loads was depending on him. They may be five against five hundred, but, by golly, Gerald was going to put up the fight of his life.

'The tarpaulin!' he yelled, running back towards the security administrators. 'Pull it down! Stretch it across the entrance to Um Bridge and get behind it!'

'What are we going to do?' asked a trembling Terence, the tallest of the administrators. 'We've only got our notebooks and pens. We've got nothing to defend ourselves with.'

'I've got a small rubber ball!' yelled a slim, blonde-haired woman called Kirsten Lea, reaching into her pocket and pulling it out. 'It's actually my cat's. But Criminal Elements are notably stupid. Perhaps I could use it to distract them?'

'Yes!' chipped in Michael, a balding man with fat lips. 'I have a multicoloured jumper on under my coat. I could use it to confuse them!'

'Or,' said Alice, a delicate-looking woman with razor-sharp cheeks, 'we could just use that pile of weapons there.' She pointed towards a large wooden box with glass doors set into the bridge entrance wall. It had a sign on it that read:

IN CASE OF ATTACK BREAK GLASS

'I'm no expert but I think they might be more effective.'

'Good thinking, Alice,' said Gerald, bending down and smashing the glass of the cupboard with a stone. More rocks were being thrown, but they were now bouncing off the tarpaulin, which had been pulled down good and tight in front of them. 'Here,' he said, passing back the weapons. 'There's a couple of clubs, a sword, a cane and an inflated pig's bladder on a stick. Who wants what?'

The four security administrators divided the weapons between them, leaving Gerald with the flimsy-looking pig's bladder. He stood, silently, and stared at it, while listening to the rocks ricocheting off the tarpaulin. Then he tightened his jaw and looked up at his companions.

'When we pledged our allegiance to the Cooper Office for People Who Owe Loads, we promised that we would do our best. I don't expect they envisaged a scenario in which administrative staff would find themselves at the sharp end of a violent conflict, yet here we are. We are only five, but we have the hearts of hundreds. We shall not waver. We shall not give in. We were sent here to protect this bridge and protect it we shall. Ladies and gents, it has been an honour to work beside you and it shall be an honour to fight beside you! Now stand strong! And spare nothing!'

Gerald's moment of greatness had arrived. Taking a quick peek round the edge of the tarpaulin he could just make out the mighty force of the Criminal Elements gathering. Barbu, he noticed, was gesturing towards their stronghold.

Gerald gulped. 'Are you ready?' he asked the four standing close behind him. They all nodded and, without saying a word, the five of them gathered into a group embrace. 'This is it,' whispered Gerald, gripping the handle of his pig's bladder tightly. 'On my count . . . one . . . two . . . thr—'

A large fist came crashing down on the top of Gerald's head. Startled, he twirled round, saw Tully standing over him, went cross-eyed and fell to the ground. The security administrators, mouths agape, looked on in horror as five hundred Criminal Elements all ran at them, weapons aloft.

Michael, not quite knowing what to do, threw off his coat and began to dance in front of the encroaching horde. 'Woooooo!' he yelled, pointing to his chest. 'Look at the swirling colours!'

As one, the Criminal Elements stopped in their tracks, heads cocked sideways as they followed Michael's hypnotic jumper.

'It's working!' squealed Kirsten, reaching for her rubber ball.

'No,' snapped Barbu, pushing his way through to the front, 'it is not working. Seize them. Tie them up. And pick him up off the ground.'

Tully bent down and pulled Gerald to his feet by the back of his collar. He was coming to and shook his head to focus.

'Barbu D'Anvers,' he said, mustering every scrap of courage he had left in him. 'By the power of the Cooper Office for People Who Owe Loads, I forbid you from entering Rascal Rock.'

Barbu stared at him with incredulity, took the fountain pen from his coat pocket and squirted ink into Gerald's face. 'Wedgie!' he yelled, as he yanked the back of Gerald's pants high above the waistline of his trousers and then, handing him over to Tully by his underwear, shouted, 'Hang him up high, Tully! As a warning to all who come!'

Tully, taking poor Gerald by the pants, spiked them through

with a tall spear and raised him so that he was hanging six feet from the ground.

'You won't get away with this, Barbu D'Anvers!' cried Gerald, as he watched the diminutive villain cross the bridge towards Rascal Rock.

'Yes,' said a toothless woman walking below him and towards the bridge. 'He will.'

With the wind howling through his hair and the rain lashing down, Barbu D'Anvers took the last few steps across the bridge to his evil lair of old, Rascal Rock. Smirking, the tiny rogue pushed open the double doors with both hands. Flicking his wet hair from his face, he looked up slowly and in a low, evil growl said, 'Hello, money. I'm home.'

Yes. You're right. It *is* awful.

Chapter 19

Wilma was munching on a corn crumble and staring up at the two Clue Boards she'd assembled in Theodore's study. To the left was the Clue Board she'd assembled earlier, which she'd now named the Case of the Masked Man. To the right was her old Clue Board for the Case of the Missing Relatives. One was smothered in pins and arrows, a picture-fit Wilma had drawn of the Masked Man (waving from a roof), the smoke-bomb fragment, a bit of crushed widdybug, the torn poster, a miniature delivery map and a few goat hairs. All arrows were pointing to Mouse as the Prime Suspect, while pinned to a corner was another hand-drawn picture of Farmer Hurl, who Wilma had labelled 'shifty'. The only new clue Wilma had for the Case of the Missing Relatives was the lichen found on the message in the bottle and the possibility that they were trapped in a damp cave. Wilma sighed. There was still a lot of working out to do for both mysteries.

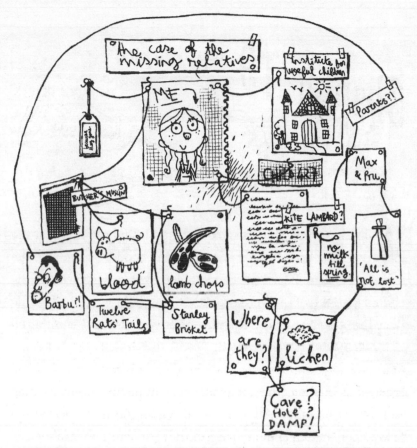

'What's that thing,' said Wilma, twirling round to face Theodore, who was sitting at his desk making notes, 'where you tiptoe backwards to find stuff out?'

Theodore, still writing, glanced up and said, 'Retracing your steps, Wilma. That's where you try to go back as far as you can in

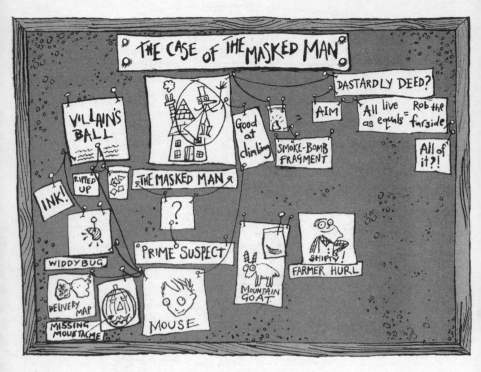

order to establish a chain of events.' He stopped and put the top back on his fountain pen. 'That's not a real chain,' he added, as he watched Wilma chew her lip in thought. 'It's a metaphorical chain.' He paused again. 'A symbol used to explain something else.'

Wilma screwed her nose up. 'So a real chain is quite long and linky. And sometimes crimes are long and linky. So the metaphorical bit is that the real chain is sort of like the clue chain and when I'm thinking about solving crimes I should think about all the things that link the beginning to the end.'

'Exactly.'

Wilma beamed with pride. She was definitely getting better at this detective business. 'Have we tried retracing our steps with the case of the Masked Man?' Wilma asked, chewing the end of her pencil thoughtfully.

'I was just recapping on where we're up to. Inspector Lemone and Captain Brock have been out all night trying to find Mouse. Lemone's staking out Emued Farm to see if he returns. Captain Brock and the 2nd Hawks Brigade have been patrolling the Great Wall. And in a moment I shall collect Glenda, gather the troops and head over to the Final Naming Ceremony. We can only hope that the Criminal Elements have been successfully trapped on the Lowside out of harm's way.'

'What about searching for Max and Pru? What if they're trapped over there too?' said Wilma. 'We can't give up, not now we've found the message.'

Theodore sat back in his chair, and turned his face towards the window. There was a sadness about him that Wilma had never seen before and she fell silent, sensing that this was a matter of some gravity.

'There's something I have to tell you, Wilma. Eleven years ago, I met a wonderful woman named Betty Boolon.

171

She was a Farsider. Her father ran the shoehorn mill over in Arewenearlythereyet. I was still a junior detective, green and untested. I was in my final year at the Academy. My mentor, Anthony Amber, had retired the year previously and Pru Lambard, Kite's elder sister, had taken over as headmistress. She had just got married to my best friend, Max Blades. He specialized in espionage. A brilliant man, brave and honest. Betty's father didn't approve of our courting. I was a Lowsider and was yet to make my name as a proper detective. So we were married in secret. But on the first day of our honeymoon Betty went missing. She completely vanished. I searched everywhere, questioned everybody, but it was as if she had never existed. I was out of my mind with worry and wasn't able to think straight so Max and Pru stepped in. They decided that the only way to find out what had happened to Betty was to go undercover as Criminal Elements. So that's what they did. They left for the Lowside and I haven't seen them since.'

'So they went missing looking for someone else who was missing. That's a lot of missing.'

'Yes, Wilma,' nodded Theodore. 'And then I searched again for years, trying to find my brave friends, but every new turn has led to a dead end. So . . . I am delighted to have this new clue – I just don't want you to get your hopes up too high. It can be . . . heartbreaking.'

'But if Max and Pru might still be alive,' suggested Wilma hopefully, 'that means Betty might still be alive too, right?'

Mr Goodman took a deep breath. 'I can only hope that—'

As is often the way with small tender moments, they are often broken by someone clattering in and ruining them, and in this instance that person was Inspector Lemone.

'No sign of the dirty beggar!' he yelled, storming in through the study door. 'I'm at my wits' end, Goodman. I haven't eaten in at least an hour. Oh, thank Cooper! Corn crumbles!' Diving on to the plate of biscuits, he stuffed four of them into his cheeks. He closed his eyes and sighed as he chewed and then, exhausted, slumped into the armchair next to the fireplace. 'Waited all night. No sign of the fellow,' mumbled Lemone, mouth still full. 'Reckon our visit yesterday must have spooked him. He'll be laying low somewhere, I'll wager.'

'Of course, we may have got lucky,' said Theodore, standing and reaching for his overcoat. 'If Mouse is the Masked Man, his absence may be because he's stuck on the Lowside, hopefully where he can do no harm. That would explain why we can't find him. Well,' he added, glancing at his fob watch, 'it's a very important day. We need to get over to the offices of Glenda Blaize. There's a lot to organize today and we need to be on full alert until six o'clock, when the Final Naming Ceremony will

173

begin. Wilma, I want you to run over to the Great Gate and tell Captain Brock we'll be escorting the Cooperate General to the ceremony and that he and a few of his men should meet us over there when the time comes, by the old oak, in case of trouble. And, Wilma . . . you're to come back with him, do you understand? I don't want you to try anything on your own.'

Wilma nodded reluctantly. If she only knew WHAT to try. 'Come on, Pickle, let's go,' she said, giving the dozy hound a small nudge.

Pickle stood, yawned and, giving himself a good shake, followed Wilma as she scampered from the study.

'OK,' she whispered, as they ran down the corridor and out through the kitchen, 'we'll give Captain Brock the message and then, somehow, we'll get into the Lowside. The answer to all of this must be there. I just *know* it. And if we get the Case of the Masked Man dusted and done we can get back to finding Mr Goodman's friends and my maybe-parents sooner!'

Wilma kicked a stone up the road as she and Pickle ran towards the Great Wall. A cordon had been set up around the border gate so that Captain Brock and his men could stand inside it and stare at the wall without distraction and ensure that no Criminal Elements penetrated the Farside defences before or during the Final Naming Ceremony. The barrier was a good two hundred feet from the border and people had gathered at its edge, some staring up at the rim of the wall, others standing in groups discussing the startling turn of events. A few border traders were unpacking boxes from carts, unable to make their deliveries into the Lowside, and it was among them that Wilma suddenly caught sight of someone. Standing outside the weighing office, arms folded, whistling and as bold as brass – it was Mouse!

'Don't give the game away, Pickle,' Wilma said, from the corner of her mouth, skidding to a halt and pressing herself against a wall, 'but suspect number one is in our sights.'

Mouse, parcel in one hand, had now stopped at a sausagenut stall and was waiting while the vendor wrapped the just cooked crispy snack into a cone of brown paper. He handed over a few groggles, and took a bite from the round sausagenut. Pickle watched jealously as thick yellow mustard squirted from its centre splattering his lips.

Wilma wasn't quite sure what to do for the best. Their prime suspect was in her line of vision but she couldn't tackle him on her own. As soon as he moved off, she reasoned, she'd see which way he was heading and then alert Captain Brock and his men. She looked around for the leader of the 2nd Hawks Brigade, then looked back again in the direction of the sausagenut stall.

'Oh no,' she wailed. 'He's gone! Quickly, Pickle,' she

added, leaping up, 'we mustn't lose him!'

They ran in the direction they'd last seen Mouse, desperately searching for him, but there was no sign of the yard lad anywhere.

Then Pickle gave out a small *whirrup*. Looking up at Wilma, he bounced a little on the spot and nudged his nose towards something thick and yellow on the floor.

'The mustard!' declared Wilma, seeing what he was pointing at. 'Good work, Pickle! You might just have saved the day!'

As any veterinary surgeon will tell you, dogs can't grin. Not because their anatomy precludes it, but because they like to maintain a hard facade. It's the same with security guards and women who work in wool shops. But Pickle felt like grinning and that's all you need to know.

To Wilma's delight, there was a trail of small dollops of mustard leading off towards the Gate cordon. People were beginning to head into central Coop to watch the Final Naming Ceremony and enjoy the festivities. Wilma jumped from one smudge of mustard to the next, each one a little smaller than the one before. The last one was nothing more than a speck, and without Pickle's keen sense of smell she might have missed it. Now what? Wilma stopped and looked around. She was now directly opposite the closed Great Gate and she could see Captain Brock and his men quite clearly. To her right was a group of Gabbler Boys, dressed in traditional costume, rehearsing the Island Hop, an overly intricate dance performed at all public Cooperan gatherings. To her left was a row of stationary carriages and a gated area where horses and mules were being rested. Suddenly, from behind one of the horses, up popped Mouse. He was lifting a saddle on to the back of a brown pony with a blond mane. Wilma had to think fast. Defying every law in the book, Wilma ducked under the cordon and ran as fast as she could towards Captain Brock.

'Ho there!' called one of the 2nd Hawks Brigade, whose job it was to try to watch things from the back of his head. 'Stand fast! Cordon breached!'

As one, Captain Brock and the other soldiers all turned sharply. Captain Brock, who did not take rule-breaking lightly, strode towards the young apprentice, his face dark and serious.

'Wilma,' he said, in a low, stern tone. 'What you've done is highly irregular. You know the rules. We must keep our eyes on the wall.'

'Never mind that,' panted Wilma, near breathless. 'I've seen Mouse – the Masked Man suspect. And he's over there, saddling that horse!'

Captain Brock's eyes, which were trained to move quicker than a speeding bullet, shot to the direction in which Wilma pointed. 'I have the fellow in my sights,' he whispered, shifting Wilma from his path. 'You stay here. Hawks! Gently does it! We have him. Now let's take him in.'

Wilma watched, still catching her breath, as the Hawks Brigade sped silently towards the fenced paddock. Like lions creeping in for the kill, they surrounded the enclosure, low to the ground and out of sight, all the while focused on their prey. Mouse, Wilma noticed, was utterly oblivious, and as he buckled his stirrups Captain Brock, in the blink of an eye, leaped up from behind and apprehended him. Wilma felt a surge of relief run through her. She couldn't hear what was being said, but she could see Mouse, shocked and wriggling. Two soldiers appeared and, taking hold of Mouse by the arms, marched him towards the Squadron Carriage. Bundling Mouse into the back of it, they all jumped aboard and before Wilma could spit or whistle they were gone, speeding away from the depot in a plume of dust.

She blinked. It had all happened so fast she had barely had time to register it. And then she realized – she was now the only person manning the Great Gate. She swallowed, turned and stared up at it.

It was then that she noticed . . . at the far end of the Great Wall . . . a grate in the floor before it was moving! To Wilma's horror, not one but *two* Criminal Elements crawled out from the manhole beneath it. One was burly and bald, while the other was a scrawny stick of a man, slightly cross-eyed. Wilma looked away, as if she hadn't seen them, in case they looked over.

'Well, that was easy,' she heard the bigger one say. 'Him were right. Got the tools?'

'Yeah,' said the smaller one, 'hidden under my jacket. Best get this lid back in place. We can have this done and be back at Rascal's Rock in an hour.'

Wilma's eyes widened. An underground route to the Lowside? To Rascal Rock? That was Barbu D'Anvers's old lair!

There will be many things that adults will warn you about over the years — not running with scissors, not drinking bleach and, if you can, avoiding putting your head in a lion's mouth. Another thing they might tell you is that if you ever see men of dubious description climbing secretly from holes in the ground and their starting point was anywhere of vaguely evil origin, then you'd be safe to assume that they're probably up to no good.

'Maybe I should run back to Cooper and find Mr Goodman and tell him?' said Wilma. 'Or . . .' she began, chewing her lip, 'I could go down that hole and see what I find at Rascal Rock. Maybe Barbu does have something to do with this Masked Man business, after all. And we can help wrap the mystery up quicker. What do you think to that, Pickle?'

Pickle knew exactly what he thought, but, being unable to speak, he was at a terrible disadvantage. This was, of course, the worst possible idea for a ten-year-old girl to have. The absolute worst. Yet here they were – running over to a manhole that led to a tunnel that would almost certainly lead to a whole host of Criminal Elements and dangerous scenarios. But Pickle couldn't say that. All he could say was, 'Woof.'

'I agree,' said Wilma, with a nod, misunderstanding him entirely. 'Let's go!'

And as Wilma ran back in the direction of the alley and the dark, foreboding hole in the ground, all Pickle could think was that it was a grave oversight that no one had ever taught dogs to talk.

A ten-year-old girl thinking she can solve this all on her own and scamper off into a place teeming with Criminal Elements? If you are experiencing feelings of intense anxiety, this is entirely normal. It's all about to go TERRIBLY wrong.

Chapter 20

Inspector Lemone was extremely fretful and since arriving at the Final Naming Ceremony had been eating corn crumbles non-stop. This seemed to help. Even Theodore, the usually calm and composed detective, was fidgeting and kept looking around nervously.

'Well,' said Glenda, 'we've done everything we could. Now we just have to sit tight and hope nothing goes wrong.'

Theodore looked at his fob watch and frowned. 'Where's Wilma?' he mumbled to himself. 'She should be here by now.'

'You don't have any spare biscuits on you, do you?' asked Lemone, eating the last corn crumble in his pocket. 'I find they settle the nerves.'

'I've got some mumblebugs,' answered Glenda, holding up a dish of boiled sweets from a table next to her. 'They're a bit stuck together. You might have to chip them apart.'

'Not to worry,' answered Lemone, 'I'll just . . . oh. They really *are* all stuck together. I suppose I can try to get them in all at once. Don't mind me.'

Theodore looked on as his nervous colleague tried to stuff a congealed pyramid of rock-hard sweets into his mouth in one go. It was a bit like watching a snake trying to eat an occasional table.

Behind them, on the stage, the ceremony entertainments were still in full swing. Five children had taken up their positions and were singing a plaintive song about vegetable patches and how every carrot, turnip and potato leaves the soil only to be roasted, boiled or chopped. It was rather bleak, not least because the middle child, dressed as a courgette, was sobbing loudly at the prospect of being lightly fried in butter.

Theodore looked out over the crowd, his moustache twitching anxiously. Even though the Great Gate had been closed, with the Masked Man still at large, it was hard to relax. That said, with the Criminal Elements now held within the Lowside, maybe they *had* managed to avert disaster? But there was something niggling away in the back of Theodore's mind. Some doubt. His experienced detective's hunch was telling him they weren't out of the woods. Not by a long shot.

The citizens of Cooper, oblivious to the troubles that beset their most famous and serious detective, were as excited as they'd been at the last two ceremonies, and the plaza was buzzing with all the sounds of an expectant crowd. Suddenly, Theodore caught sight of the 2nd Hawks Brigade carriage thundering up the avenue behind them. 'At last. Captain Brock. Look sharp, Lemone.'

Inspector Lemone, already near his wits' end with worry and still trying to suck his way through the hard fist of boiled sweets in his mouth, threw a startled look in Theodore's direction.

'Buffpggh ghgnnn gngngn?' he spluttered as he struggled to run after him.

The 2nd Hawks Brigade carriage skidded to a halt. From the front leaped Captain Brock who strode purposefully towards Theodore and Lemone.

'We have him, Mr Goodman!' he called out. 'Your Masked Man Your apprentice spotted him. We apprehended him as soon as we could and brought him straight to you.'

Behind Captain Brock, two of his men were bundling Mouse down from the carriage. He was still struggling and his eyes were wild and troubled.

Theodore stepped towards him. 'Let him go, please,' he said sternly.

'Isn't that unwise?' asked Brock, his eyes boring into Mouse's face. 'He is the man you've been looking for. And, if he is who you think he is, he's nippy on his feet.'

'Until proven guilty, I prefer a man to be standing upright, as he should be.'

Captain Brock nodded and the two soldiers who held Mouse in a tight restraint suddenly let him go.

'What's this about?' the young man yelled angrily, as he rubbed feeling back into his arms. 'I was minding my own business! Grabbed off the street! I've still got deliveries to make! I'll be in trouble up the farm! That gate nonsense has already slowed me down – now this!'

Theodore squared his shoulders and gave the young man standing before him a good long look. His eyes were blazing blue, his cheeks brown from working outside. His physique was strong, as you would expect from someone who helped out on a farm, and his gaze, full of anger, confusion and alarm, was all the same steady and true.

'Sometimes,' Theodore began, 'circumstances can point the finger of suspicion in one very clear direction. We have been tracking a fellow known only as the Masked Man, an idealist who thinks he can turn this island upside down overnight. His motives,' Theodore continued, twitching his moustache, 'may be noble but his methods are not.'

'What has this got to do with me?' asked Mouse, shaking his head. 'I never even heard of no Masked Man.'

'Gnnghnnnn!' shouted Lemone, standing behind Theodore's shoulder. 'Ggngngh gnnngn!'

Mouse blinked. 'What did he say?'

Theodore persisted. 'Young man, you had access to the widdybug that made the ink for the Masked Man's poster. You have no fear of heights, as witnessed by your fixing of the chimney pot. You were making mumblebugs, the sweet that Inspector Lemone is trying to chew right now, the key ingredient of which is lactose, also a vital component in the construction of smoke bombs. A Ten-Annual Election poster was found torn up outside your quarters and you make false moustaches, one of which may have been worn as part of the Masked Man's disguise. Each of these things individually may be quite innocent, but the fact that *all* these elements point to you is overwhelming. Now what have you to say about that?'

Mouse stood for a moment in perplexed thought. 'I do sometimes work over the blue-cabbage patch, collect up the widdybugs, but I don't make the ink. And I wouldn't know how to make a poster if I tried. I am good with heights, but then everyone who works on the farm is. We always have to be up trees and whatnots. And, as for sweets, I might have eaten a few, but I don't make them. That's someone else. I just make the savoury lumps. Look, I got a bag here.'

'I'll take that,' said Inspector Lemone, finally swallowing the last of the mumblebugs. Reaching forward he took the small paper bag of savoury lumps and peered inside. 'He's not lying, Goodman,' he said, looking a little perplexed. 'There are savoury lumps in here. I'll just double-check.'

Inspector Lemone turned the bag upside down and tipped the entire contents into his mouth.

'That could be considered evidence!' said Goodman, looking a little exasperated.

'Not any more,' mumbled Lemone, chewing frantically.

'I do make moustaches and wigs and stuff. But they're for the plays at the museum. It's just a hobby. I can't even wear them. The goat hair brings me up in a rash. I have to wear gloves when I work with it. And as for the ripped poster. Well. I'd rather not say. But it wasn't me.'

Theodore's jaw tightened; his eyes narrowed. 'You know who ripped up that poster?'

'And I will not tell,' said the lad, standing taller.

Theodore gripped him firmly by the forearm and fixed him with a piercing gaze. 'Was it your employer? Cicatrise Hurl? Forget your allegiance! Lives may depend on it!'

Mouse's head fell to his chest. He nodded quickly, once, and then looked ashamed. 'He is a very great man, Mr Goodman,' he said quietly.

A small silence fell as Theodore stood, deep in thought.

'Gentlemen,' he said at last, turning to his companions, 'we have been chasing the wrong man.'

'It was Farmer Hurl all along?' Inspector Lemone scraped a hand exasperatedly down his face. 'Oh lawks. It's all gone wonky.'

'Wonky . . .' repeated Theodore, his face filled with worry. 'Captain Brock . . . where is Wilma?'

But Captain Brock had no idea.

Yet we do, don't we, readers? She's down a dark hole and heading into a den of vipers. Someone send the cavalry. Quick!

187

Chapter 21

Someone was coming. Wilma pressed herself into a dark alcove, Pickle tucking in close behind her. The manhole had dropped down into a long, dark tunnel. There was a strong smell of damp and mud and, apart from the odd flaming torch set into the wall, it was pitch black. At first, Wilma had thought the small ball of light behind them was another fixed torch, but, as it swayed gently from side to side, she realized it was being carried. Somebody was making their way towards them — and closing.

Wilma's heart thumped in her chest and she thought, again, of Mr Goodman's words to her. '*I don't want you to try anything on your own . . .*' She looked down at Pickle who, sensing her gaze, stared devotedly back at her. As long as she had him, she thought, she'd never be alone. They were in it together. Through thick and thin.

She could hear footsteps and low, tuneless whistling. She pressed her back hard against the wall, longing for the shadows to swallow her and Pickle up and keep them safe. The travelling orb of light was almost upon them now and, as it crept along the floor and slithered up the walls, Wilma felt herself being slowly illuminated. The light was seeping into every nook and cranny. She mustn't move. Not one muscle. If she managed to keep still, there was every chance that whoever it was would simply not see her or her beagle and pass by.

Pickle, always protective, slipped quietly in front of her and crouched low and near. Wilma could feel his soft fur against her leg and, despite the fear racing through her, it was a comfort to know that her brave beagle was by her side. The light grew stronger still, the footsteps louder and Wilma, grimacing, tried to press herself into the small patch of dark that clung to the deepest corner of the alcove. As the flaming torch came into view, she could feel its heat on her cheeks. She was terrified. If she was found now, all would be lost. First a hand, then an arm, then the body of a man heaved into view. It was Tully!

Wilma's eyes widened, but still she had to be silent. The warm glow of the torch danced over her face. If Tully turned his head now, he would see her. She could feel Pickle tensing below her, the hair on the back of his neck instinctively rising. The tension was unbearable, but seconds later Tully, oblivious to their presence and lost in the song he was whistling, passed them by.

She waited a moment then, when there was a safe distance between them, she crept slowly after him down the tunnel, Pickle close at her heels. She didn't have to explain to him what they were doing – they would let Barbu's stupid henchman lead them straight to wherever the Criminal Elements were hiding.

The tunnel wove onward, narrowing in places, turning this way then that, until they reached a short set of steps leading up to a thick wooden door. They waited till they heard Tully go through it, then crept to the door and listened. Wilma could hear muffled voices.

'It's them. I can hear Barbu talking to Janty,' she whispered to Pickle. 'I think they're getting ready to go somewhere.'

Barbu was standing in front of a full-length mirror, head back and laughing. 'They're going to have the shock of their lives!' he guffawed, primping a purple silk cravat. 'NEVER underestimate a master villain! We're sneaky! We're despicable! Everything is going according to plan. Now all we have to do is make our way into the Farside and seal the deal! Hopefully the Masked Man will catch up with us there too.'

Janty, who was leaning against the wall to Barbu's left, gave a small shrug. 'My father always used to say it was unwise to count chickens before they hatched. He said even the greatest plans can go awry.'

Barbu twirled on the spot to glare at his young apprentice. 'Who cares what your father thought?' he snapped cruelly. 'He's dead. Remember?'

Janty's face hardened, but he knew better than to answer back. He bit his lip and remained silent. His father used to say, 'Be careful what you wish for too.' Here Janty was, in Rascal Rock, on the cusp of his master's most daring plan. He should have been filled with excitement, but instead he felt deadened and hollow. This was not the life he had hoped for.

'Where's my cape?' yelled Barbu, looking around the room petulantly. 'If I am going to take over this island once and for all, I need to look fabulous and regal. Especially if the Masked Man turns up. I can't have him stealing my thunder.'

'I think it's upstairs, master,' said Janty quietly, his head still bowed.

Barbu gave an exasperated sigh. 'Hasn't Tully gone up there? TULLLYYYYYY?' he called. 'Ugh,' he heaved. 'FINE. Come on. Let's go up and fetch it. We have to leave soon anyway. Don't DAWDLE!'

Wilma, still standing on the other side of the door, had heard everything. She waited for a few moments and then, when she

191

was sure they had gone, slowly and carefully pushed down on the handle and inched the door open. 'Come on, Pickle,' she whispered, poking her nose through into the room, 'the coast is clear. Let's see what we can find out.'

The room was sparsely decorated and, other than the full-length mirror leaning against the wall opposite, there was no other furniture in the room to speak of. What there was, however, was the rubbishy cow Wilma had seen the day before, at the parade. Wilma frowned. What was that doing here? Not only that, but in the far corner of the room Wilma could see three milk-churn outfits piled up against each other . . .

Still cautious of making a noise, Wilma tiptoed carefully to the far flank of the wooden cow and peered around to take a closer look. Her hand shot to her mouth as she tried to stifle a gasp. The rear side of the cow had a removable panel and hidden inside it was something that looked exactly like the Grand Tombola! Wilma couldn't quite take in what she was seeing. How could this be? She'd seen the Grand Tombola with her own two eyes safe behind the curtains. How was it now here? How had they stolen it? And what were they doing with it?

She stood back and tried to think, but then she caught sight of the floor around her. It was covered in tiny scraps of paper. Bending down, she picked one up and turned it over to read.

'Thorn Mayer,' she read. She picked up another . . . 'Logan

Dent . . .' And another . . . 'Viner Ronson. Oh my . . .' The penny was starting to drop. And then she saw it, a small box of other scraps of paper, tucked into the corner inside the cow. Trembling, she bent down again and pulled a handful of paper strips from it. She looked at them. What she saw was the worst thing imaginable. She shook her head. 'Oh no,' she whispered, near to tears. 'We have to get back to the Farside at once, Pickle . . .'

'I don't think there's any chance of that happening,' said a voice from the doorway in front of her.

Wilma froze. It was Barbu D'Anvers, with Janty by his side. The papers in her hand fell to the floor.

Barbu cast an eye downward in their direction. 'I see you are aware of our plans . . .' he began with a low sneer. 'It's only a pity that you are in no position to do anything to prevent them,' he added with an evil laugh.

Wilma's voice caught in her throat as she stumbled backwards. 'You . . . you won't get away with this,' she stuttered, looking around quickly for something with which to protect herself.

'That's what you think,' said Barbu, flicking back the edge of his cape to reveal a small silver pistol at his belt. 'But I think you'll find I'm getting away with it as we speak. What's important to me now is that you don't go anywhere. And there's

193

only one way to ensure that, really, isn't there? I should have killed you when I first had the chance. You're nothing more than a meddling orphan. No one will miss you.'

Barbu pulled out his pistol, aiming it straight at the terrified little girl. Pickle let out a low growl.

'You might think it's a great pity that you have nobody to cry out to, nobody to help you, but this is exactly how I prefer it. I shoot my pistol, you die and I never have to think about you again.' He cocked the firing mechanism. Pickle's growl grew louder.

Wilma shook her head, her heart beating wildly. 'Janty,' she said, terror in her eyes. 'Help me. Please.'

The young boy, standing rigid behind his master, stared unblinking into Wilma's eyes. But inside he was in turmoil. Wilma had been nothing but kind to him and here she was, about to be killed by a man he didn't even like, let alone respect.

'*Help me!*' mocked Barbu, an evil smirk spreading across his face. '*Pleeeeease* . . . No, Wilma Tenderfoot. It's time for you to *die!*'

Barbu's finger tightened on the trigger, but as he shot his pistol Janty, in a moment of blinding conscience, grabbed his forearm to stop him. But it was too late. The bullet flew from Barbu's gun, heading straight for Wilma. She shut her eyes, her arms instinctively rising up to protect herself, but she knew it was hopeless. The bullet was going to hit her.

She waited for the pain to come.

But it didn't.

Instead, she heard a whimper and a thud on the floor in front of her. Wilma opened her eyes and looking down at her feet saw Pickle, blood trickling from a bullet wound in his chest. As the gun had sounded, Pickle had leaped up to protect her, taking the bullet in his own body. Wilma fell to her knees, all the air gone from her lungs, and held her beloved beagle in her arms. Pickle, his life already ebbing away, took a long, last look at his best friend, and with one gentle whimper he closed his eyes forever.

Chapter 22

'No!' cried Wilma, tears pouring forth. 'Not Pickle! He can't be dead, he can't!'

She had never felt pain like it. Pickle was dead. Her constant companion, her first and forever friend, gone. As she cradled the body of her beloved beagle, she sobbed, grief-stricken, no thought for anything other than him.

Barbu, having shaken off Janty, aimed his gun at her once more. 'You may have escaped one bullet, but you shan't escape a second,' he shouted.

Wilma looked up, tears cascading down her cheeks. Barbu D'Anvers had killed her best friend. A ball of rage gathered in the pit of her stomach and she suddenly leaped, with no thought of her own safety, to grab the evil villain by the wrist, sending the gun catapulting through the air. Caught off guard, Barbu stumbled backwards.

'You won't get away again, Wilma Tenderfoot!' the villain screamed. 'Where's my gun? Janty! Find my gun!'

Wilma, realizing that her life was still in dreadful danger, scooped Pickle's body up into her arms and ran back out into the tunnel. But Pickle's body was heavy and she couldn't run as fast as she ordinarily might. Her breath caught in her throat, tears blinded her and she could hear Barbu screaming at Janty to give chase. Then footsteps running behind her. But she was so tired. If she could just stop and catch her breath . . . It was more than that too; it felt as if something inside her had died. She didn't want to run any more. Her footfalls slowed to a walk then slowed again to a dead halt. She leaned up against the tunnel wall and pressed her face to Pickle's body, his fur still warm to her touch. She was utterly heartbroken.

'Let them find me and kill me,' she whispered into Pickle's fur. 'I just want to be where you are.'

The running footsteps behind her had skidded to a halt. Wilma looked up, red-eyed, her bottom lip trembling. Janty was staring down at her, his chest heaving. Wilma wiped the tears from her eyes with the back of one hand and stood tall, lifting Pickle so that he lay with his head resting on her shoulder.

'I don't care what you do to me,' she said, with a small shake of her head. 'Take me back to him. Let him kill me. I don't care any more.'

Janty stared back at Wilma. She looked broken and hollow, he thought. The light had gone from her eyes. And as she clasped Pickle's lifeless body something tugged at his heart.

Barbu yelled again: 'Have you found her? Is she there?' His cries echoed down the tunnel. Janty looked away, then back again at Wilma.

Then he shouted, 'No. She's gone!'

Wilma blinked. She didn't understand. Janty placed a gentle hand on her shoulder. 'I'm sorry about your dog. I really am. Now run. Please. And don't stop running,' he urged, 'it's what Pickle would have wanted.'

'Th-thank you,' Wilma whispered, her tears coming again.

Janty was right. It WAS what Pickle would have wanted. He'd died saving her and if she didn't escape it would render his sacrifice pointless. She turned and ran again as fast as she was able. Suddenly there was something to run for – something that had now become the most important thing in the world. She had to get Pickle home.

The Final Naming Ceremony was almost at its end. The mood of the crowd was jubilant despite their recent trauma at the Great Gate, but with no sign of Wilma and the

Masked Man still unidentified a grim mood hung in the air onstage.

Glenda looked over her shoulder and frowned. 'Where's Dromley?' she asked, shaking her head. 'Honestly, the one moment in the ceremony when he'd actually be of use and he's nowhere to be seen. I'm sorry to have to impose, Mr Goodman, but could you and Inspector Lemone wheel the Grand Tombola forward for me? It's almost time to pull out the name of our next Cooperate General.'

'Of course,' answered Theodore. 'We'll bring it to the front of the stage immediately.'

'Do you think we've got away with it?' mumbled Lemone as the two of them headed towards the Grand Tombola with Kite Lambard at their side. 'I've seen no Criminal Elements and it's been nice and peaceful so far.'

'Don't speak too soon, Inspector,' answered Theodore. 'We're not out of the woods yet. With the latest revelations I'm even more sure the Masked Man is still on the Farside and potentially as impassioned as ever. Who knows what that means for the grand plan, even with the gate closed. Stay alert. And I can't relax until I know Wilma is safe – *where is she?*'

Miss Lambard nodded worriedly beside the inspector. 'But there's not much we can do at the moment – so this seems the best place to be on all counts.' She went off to position herself strategically in the crowds.

As the men lifted the Grand Tombola into place, Glenda Blaize took centre stage for the third and final time. She cleared her throat and began.

'Ten years ago, I was honoured to be named Cooper Island's Cooperate General. In that time I have come to realize that Cooper is a wondrous place. From its rolling plains in the south, to the One Small Hill in the north, our great nation is glorious and abundant. The people of Cooper, the island's beating heart, welcomed me into office with open arms. I hope that I have repaid that faith and served you as you deserve.'

A wave of polite applause rippled towards the stage. Theodore, ever watchful, scanned the crowd and out of the corner of his eye caught sight of someone – it was Janty. Theodore frowned. He shouldn't be here. Surely Janty was on the Lowside when the Great Gate was shut? Oh dear. This could only mean one thing.

'Lemone,' Theodore whispered, touching his friend lightly on the forearm, 'Two o'clock. Barbu's boy. Don't stare. Look over my shoulder as if we're chatting.'

'Two o'clock?' asked Lemone, looking at his watch. 'It's past six. Might need to get your watch to the menders.'

'No,' persisted Theodore, widening his eyes and giving the inspector an intense stare, 'not two o'clock the *time*, two o'clock the *direction* in which to look.'

Inspector Lemone shot a blank expression back. 'No idea what you're talking about, Goodman,' he whispered, leaning in. 'Two o'clock is a time. Not a direction. You sure you're feeling all right?'

Theodore tensed his jaw. 'Lemone, look at your watch. Hold it up. Do you see where the two is?' Lemone nodded. 'Now look over my shoulder in *that* direction. The direction of two o'clock on your watch.'

'Oh!' exclaimed Lemone, beaming. 'Got it now. Two o'clock. So that's over there. Well I never. Dash it all, Goodman! It *is* Barbu's boy!'

'Yes,' replied Theodore, in a low tone. 'Now look behind him and to the side. Can you see Barbu?'

Inspector Lemone narrowed his eyes and cast a look out over the crowd. 'No. He's with a man in a hood,' said Lemone, straining to see. 'He's DEFINITELY with him, he's got an arm round him now in a kind of fatherly way, or maybe it's a threatening way – I'm not sure.'

'Man in a hood? Fatherly . . . Hang on,' said Theodore, his eyes sharpening. 'What was it Wilma said about the tombola tableau . . . Oh my goodness, I think she had something right all

201

along! Janty is the son of a forger, after all, and an orphan now too—'

'Oh my,' interrupted Lemone, who up to this point had been looking completely baffled but was now turning a little white too. 'I can see Criminal Elements everywhere. They've surrounded the place, Goodman. Some of them are carrying weapons.'

'Then our worst fears are realized,' declared Theodore, taking his friend by the shoulder. 'And I'm suddenly not so sure the Masked Man is entirely to blame any more. Are you ready, Lemone? This may turn ugly.'

Lemone blinked. This was as serious a matter as he had ever found himself involved in. He swallowed and answered, 'I'll stand with you till the last breath in my body, Goodman – you know that.'

'Let's hope it doesn't come to that,' said Theodore grimly. 'Now I suggest we try to stop this Naming Ceremony before it's too late.'

But Glenda had already placed her hand deep into the ancient tombola. The crowd was cheering wildly and the noise was deafening; Theodore's calls went unheard.

He turned to Lemone and shouted, 'She can't hear me! We're going to need back-up! Fetch Captain Brock. He's in the backstage area!'

Lemone nodded and pulled back the curtain that divided the stage from the area behind it, but as he did so he gasped in shock. Tully and five other Criminal Elements were standing waiting and as they saw Lemone they descended.

'Run, Theodore!' the inspector cried, trying to hold them off. But it was no use. As Theodore made a dash to get to Glenda, Tully took him down with a swipe to the lower legs and, as he tumbled, Tully's sidekicks descended on him too. Behind the curtain, Lemone could see Captain Brock and his men tied up and surrounded as well.

This was a disaster!

'Unhand me!' cried out Theodore, struggling. 'You might just be following orders, but you're making matters far worse for yourselves!'

'Oh,' said a voice, emerging from behind Tully and the band of thugs. 'I think things are about to get far, far worse . . . all by themselves . . .'

Theodore looked up from the floor. It was Barbu, resplendent and smirking. At the front of the stage, Glenda Blaize, oblivious to the scuffles behind her, pulled out one scrap of paper from the Grand Tombola and held it aloft. The crowd roared.

'The name has been drawn!' she cried. 'And the new Cooperate General is . . .' She brought the paper closer to her face to read it. She shook her head. This couldn't be. Then, looking out to the crowd as if for help, she said weakly, 'Barbu D'Anvers.'

Haven't the last two chapters been just AWFUL?

Chapter 23

The place was in chaos. Women were screaming, men were fainting and every child in the square seemed to be wailing at the top of their voice. Criminal Elements were everywhere, brandishing all manner of weapons, and Barbu was centre stage, flanked by Tully and a small mob of thugs. Behind them, Theodore and Lemone were tied up and pinned to the floor.

'Citizens of Cooper!' cried Barbu, the wind blowing through his cape. 'I have been officially declared as the new Cooperate General! I claim my right to be sworn in by the Keeper of Cooper Law!'

Melba Toest grimaced and stepped forward gingerly.

'Don't do it!' cried a man from the crowd. 'Can't you find a law that says we don't have to have him?'

Melba shook her head. 'His name was drawn from the Grand Tombola. That means he's in charge.'

'This is the worst arrangement imaginable!' yelled someone else in the crowd. 'We haven't thought this through! We can't let our government depend on a random scrap of paper. It's madness!'

'Oh, do shut UP!' yelled Barbu. 'You know the rules! One name gets pulled out. And that name was mine.'

'But it was meant to be MINE!' came a cry from the edge of the stage. A hooded figure strode towards the diminutive villain. 'That was our arrangement. I gave you the plans to create an exact replica of the Grand Tombola. You were supposed to get it into position and fill it with MY name. Not YOURS. In return, as the new Cooperate General, I'd reinstate you at Rascal Rock and cut the Lowside some slack on the sly. You've double-dealt me.'

'Hang on a minute,' said Glenda, frowning. 'I know that voice.'

'Of course you do!' Theodore P. Goodman, the great and serious detective, might have been face down on the stage, but his voice was still as wise and true as ever. 'It's someone close to you who over the years has become so bitter and jealous of your power that he has resorted to courting known criminals to get what he wants.' Theodore craned his neck to look upward as the hooded figure before them all pulled back his hood and revealed his true self.

Mr Goodman nodded. Lemone's jaw dropped. Glenda gasped loudly.

'DROMLEY?' she yelled, her face flushed red with rage. 'What are you doing making arrangements with Barbu D'Anvers? Have you *lost your mind?*'

'I couldn't wait to see you replaced,' Dromley snapped in his former employer's direction. 'You never listened to any of my ideas for the island. Never gave me any credit. I should have been in charge! But I couldn't rely on our antiquated tombolocracy system to give me the power I deserved. Then the Masked Man arrived on the scene . . . and with the legal forces so distracted elsewhere, suddenly I saw my chance. One that would see the Grand Tombola replaced with a fake and filled with thousands of identical pieces of paper with one name on them – MINE! But I couldn't do it alone. I needed someone villainous enough to make the tombola and the switch. Villainous enough to double-cross me too, it seems!'

'But the Masked Man,' Lemone blustered.

'In fact,' Theodore turned to his friend, bound on the floor beside him, 'I don't think the Masked Man had much to do with all this in the end, after all. I—'

Suddenly there was a loud cry from above the stage.

'Speak of the devil,' Glenda Blaize cried out.

It was indeed the Masked Man, crouching at the top of the

arch above the stage! Swinging on one of the velvet curtains, he leaped nimbly down to land neatly in front of Dromley. He turned to the crowd. In particular he seemed to turn towards a dashing figure at the front of the crowd before the stage.

'This was not what I wanted. Not like this,' the Masked Man began.

'But – but how?' burbled Inspector Lemone looking back and forth between the Masked Man on the stage and Cicatrise Hurl, standing at the front of the crowd staring up. 'The Masked Man and the Masked Man unmasked in the same place at the same time as two different people?'

Theodore glanced at Lemone knowingly. 'Farmer Hurl is not the Masked Man and he never was. Remember how he told us that first time we met him that he didn't like to get his hands dirty?'

'But who?' wailed the inspector, literally cross-eyed with confusion.

'I must take responsibility for my part in this unfortunate sequence of events,' the Masked Man was saying now. 'It was I who sparked the flames of mutiny. I wanted equality and justice for the Lowside – it wasn't right that their names were excluded from the tombola draw – but what started out as an ill-conceived plan to rob the Farside of its riches and give to the poor has turned into something much more sinister. And now it's all gone wrong. The gate that divides this great country is shut because of me. Barbu D'Anvers is in charge because of me. I didn't mean for it to be like this . . .'

'Who is it, Goodman?' Lemone asked again.

'Someone whose head has been filled with contrary ideas about the election,' began Theodore, his eyes ablaze, 'whose romantic notions about the island, and one person in particular, have been driving every action. Someone who had access to the ink, the lactose, the false moustaches. Someone with an inclination for drama and stage effects. Someone who, like Mouse, would do anything for Cicatrise Hurl. Though not out of duty this time. Out of adoration. She is in love with him.'

Barbu stared incredulously. He couldn't quite believe his ears and then, as he stared harder, he couldn't quite believe his eyes.

'SHE?' he snapped suddenly as Mr Goodman's words sunk in. Then, 'His moustache . . . It's coming off . . .' he added disbelievingly.

The tiny villain strode forward and with one deft movement yanked off the Masked Man's mask and moustache. A gasp went up from the crowd.

'UGH,' Barbu sneered. 'He *is* a she.' His criminal sidekicks began to boo. 'Good job you've got me, eh?' Barbu preened. 'After all these decades I've given you the Farside at last.' The Criminal Elements began to cheer again.

Brenda Blaize, finally unmasked, stared imploringly towards her sister. 'I just wanted the island to be equal!' she cried. 'I didn't want Cooper to be divided! And now it's more divided than ever!'

'Oh, Brenda,' shouted up Cicatrise. 'I didn't agree with the election. Never have. But you shouldn't have done this!'

'You fool, Brenda,' said Glenda, shaking her head. 'You sparked a manhunt that led Goodman and his troops a merry dance and in keeping them tied up with *that* you've handed the island to a villain on a plate! What were you thinking?'

Brenda spun back round and grabbed Barbu by the arm. 'Please, Mr D'Anvers,' she implored. 'It's not too late. You can get the Criminal Elements to give back what they've taken. It doesn't have to be like this! You can bring good to this island! I'm begging you!'

Barbu shoved her hand away with the end of his cane. 'I have absolutely no interest in bringing good to anyone other than myself. Now shoo. Shoo over there. I have nothing further to say to you. *You* let me do what I wanted with your plan. Remember?'

'Never mind her!' yelled Dromley, persisting, 'give me what is mine, Barbu!'

Barbu turned back to Dromley and shrugged. 'You're getting nothing. Everyone hates a weasel. And get off my stage,'

210

he added, shoving him in the stomach forcibly with his cane. 'Nobody steals my thunder. Especially not a man in a GHASTLY-smelling sack.'

Dromley, toppling backwards, fell over a small plinth at the side of the stage. He scrabbled, undignified, to his feet and realized he was face to face with Glenda.

'Idiot,' she spat.

'Now get on with the swearing in,' yelled Barbu.

Melba, her hands shaking, lifted *The Golden Book of Cooper* – a large, heavy volume containing all the legends of the island. It was on this that Barbu would have to swear to uphold Cooper's traditions.

'Barbu D'Anvers,' began Melba, her voice weak and reluctant, 'you have been declared as the Cooperate General of Cooper. Raise your right hand, place it on the book and repeat after me . . . I hereby promise—'

'I don't do promises. Next bit . . .' snapped Barbu.

Melba blinked. 'But you're supposed to promise to uphold the ancient traditions of the island and to preserve them for future generations,' she began, in protest.

'NEXT BIT!' yelled Barbu.

Melba swallowed. 'I will fight for truth and justice—'

'No. Not doing that. Next bit,' Barbu snapped again.

'And preserve the well-being of all Cooper's citizens—'

'*All* of them? Are you quite mad? NO. Right. Is that it? Am I sworn in?'

'But he didn't swear to *anything!*' shouted a red-faced woman in the crowd. 'That means it's not legal, doesn't it?'

Melba looked down and shook her head regretfully. 'I don't think it does. No one's ever refused to swear in properly before. Not in all of Cooper's history. We haven't got a law to cover it. This is a terrible loophole.'

'Good,' said Barbu, shoving Melba out of the way. 'That's that. I am now the Cooperate General. And in accordance with tradition I shall now pass three new laws, which shall come into effect immediately. Number one. The Grand Tombola shall be destroyed and there will never be another Ten-Annual Election ever again. Tully – set fire to it.'

Shocked gasps rang out across the plaza.

'But what does that mean?' cried out a confused-looking lad near the front of the stage.

'It *means* that I am now in charge FOREVER. New law number two – all of your money is now mine. Start handing it over. We've already got teams all over the Farside stripping it of its wealth. Now empty your pockets and give the contents to the Criminal Elements too. They've got sacks. It's perfectly straightforward. And new law number three . . . Oh, wait, let me savour this moment. Pick Theodore P. Goodman up from the floor, Tully. Bring him to me.'

'I'm just setting fire to the tombola, Mr D'Anvers,' replied
the stupid henchman, fanning a pile of smoking sticks.

'Never mind that,' barked Barbu, twirling his cane in triumph,
'I want to make this as humiliating as possible.'

Theodore, still being sat on by four thugs at the front of the
stage, was pulled to his feet and dragged towards Barbu.

'You won't get away with this, D'Anvers,' he said, struggling
to free himself.

Barbu shot him a baffled stare. 'I've already *got away with it*,
Goodman. And there's nothing you can do about it. In fact, I am
now going to make sure that there is nothing you can do about
anything EVER AGAIN.' He pressed the end of his cane sharply
into Theodore's chest and turned to the crowd. 'And, for my
last election law, my gift to you, Cooper! Theodore P. Goodman
shall be stripped of his detective's badge!'

Barbu leaned in and pulled Theodore's golden seal of office
from the inside lapel of his overcoat. Sneering, he held it aloft.
'He's finished! You're *all* finished! Ah ha ha ha! HA HA HA HA
HA HA HA!'

The crowd stared up in silence as their new leader crowed
over them. Theodore's head fell towards his chest, his arms
pinned tight behind his back. Behind him Lemone turned his
face away, his eyes fighting back the tears.

Wilma, exhausted and desolate, had made it back to the Central Plaza at last. She pushed her way through the crowds towards the stage, unseeing, unknowing, her dead dog heavy in her arms.

Suddenly she saw a familiar face in the crowd. It was Mrs Speckle. She was staring up at the stage and dabbing her eyes with a woollen handkerchief. Wilma, desperate for a friend, pushed her way towards her.

Mrs Speckle was as tough as they came and over the years had seen many a calamity that weaker-minded souls might have buckled under, but seeing the Great Detective debadged and Cooper's notorious villain instated as the new Cooperate General was by far the worst thing she had ever witnessed. And it was about to get worse still . . .

'Mrs Speckle,' said a weak voice by her side. The housekeeper turned, and saw Wilma, Pickle lain limply across her chest. Wilma's cheeks were tear-stained, her eyes red raw. She was a picture of despair.

Mrs Speckle, realizing instantly what had happened, lay a hand gently on Pickle's head. 'Oh no, Wilma,' she said softly, her face filled with sorrow. 'Not Pickle.' And with a heartfelt sigh she engulfed the poor child in an embrace. Wilma, finding herself at last in the arms of comfort, sobbed into Mrs Speckle's chest. It was as dark a day as the housekeeper could ever remember.

'Theodore P. Goodman!' yelled Barbu from the stage. 'You are no longer a detective. In fact, you are nothing! Toss him and his useless, fat friend from the stage.' A horrified cry went up as Theodore and Lemone were untied and pushed off the stage, Barbu's exultant expression filling the crowd with shock and horror.

Barbu gazed out over the citizens before him. 'Scum of Cooper! Things are going to change around here! All of you now work for me! Am I going to be fair? No. Am I going to be kind? No. I'm going to be *awful*. Every single one of you is going to suffer. And the best thing is I couldn't care less! Criminal Elements!' yelled Barbu. 'Bring the stolen hoard to Rascal Rock! My triumph is now complete! REVENGE IS MINE!' And, with that, he swept from the stage, his cloak flapping behind him.

Lemone heaved a terrible sigh. 'This is more awful than we could ever have imagined,' he said. 'We're beaten, Goodman. Beaten.'

Theodore, who was making his way to the back of the plaza, shook his head gravely. 'No, Lemone,' he said, his voice steady and true, 'we may be down. But we're not out.'

'Mr Goodman!' a voice called out. Theodore looked up and saw Mrs Speckle waving a hand at him. And tucked behind her Theodore saw Wilma, still carrying the lifeless body of her best friend. Without a moment's hesitation, he rushed to her side, took Pickle's body from her, handed him to Lemone and scooped her into his arms.

'He died protecting me. I can't believe he's gone. I thought Pickle would always save the day,' Wilma cried into his shoulder.

'He did, Wilma,' replied Theodore gently. 'Because you're still here.'

Can't. Get. Any. Worse.

Chapter 24

The next day they buried Pickle. The far corner of the garden at Clarissa Cottage was to be his final resting place. Inspector Lemone had made a small wooden coffin from an old vegetable box as soon as they'd got back to the cottage from the Central Plaza, and the brave beagle had been lying in it on his favourite rug ever since, with a few corn crumbles by his side, 'In case he gets hungry on his journey,' said Mrs Speckle, wiping away the tears.

That night, even after all the exhausting events of the day, Wilma had refused to go to bed, despite everyone's attempts to insist she needed rest. She just wanted to sit up in the front parlour with Pickle's body so that she could be with him for as long as possible before having to say goodbye forever. All night she sat on a small stool next to him, her face resting on the coffin's edge so that she could look at him.

*

As dawn broke, Theodore knocked gently on the parlour door. 'Mind if I come in?' he asked softly.

Wilma lifted her head from the end of Pickle's coffin, her hand still draped down inside it, and nodded. She was still snuffling, her sadness ebbing and flowing with the memories of their happy times together.

'We're all very worried about you,' said Theodore, pulling up a chair and sitting beside her.

Wilma wiped her nose with the back of her hand. 'I didn't think it was possible to feel as sad as I do. But it's like the sun has gone in forever, Mr Goodman. I don't think I shall ever smile again.'

Theodore looked up towards the window, the first rays of the morning beginning to break. 'But the great thing about the sun, Wilma,' he said softly, 'is that it does rise again, every morning. It never lets us down. Day in, day out. It reminds us that life carries on. However dreadful, however disastrous the things that beset us, the world keeps turning. I had a dog once. She was a sweet thing. A tiny Jack Russell. I could carry her around in my overcoat pocket when she was a pup. And that dog brought me more joy and happiness than I deserved. But the sad truth about animals is that we often only have them for a short period of time. They are not ours to keep. I know Pickle has been taken from you too soon, but you'll carry him with you in your heart forever and, in that respect, he hasn't gone at all. He'll always be with you.'

Theodore placed a comforting hand on his young apprentice's shoulder. Wilma chewed at her lip as the tears fell once more.

'Everyone's outside,' Theodore said tenderly. 'It's time to say your goodbyes, Wilma.'

The young apprentice hung her head and took one last long look at her best friend. His brave and noble face in profile, his paws tucked up as if in sleep, he seemed at peace. She reached into her pinafore pocket and pulled out the small luggage tag that had been tied about her wrist when she was a baby. It was the most precious thing she possessed. She held it in her hands, looked at it one last time and then, very gently, placed it inside Pickle's coffin.

'Goodbye, dear Pickle,' she gulped. 'I love you so much.'

Theodore, rising from his chair, took the top of Pickle's coffin and slid it into place. As it shut tight, Wilma squeezed her eyes closed and turned away, her bottom lip trembling.

'If it's all right with you, Wilma,' said Theodore, 'I'll ask Lemone to come in and help me carry him down the garden.'

Wilma gave a small nod and Theodore opened the parlour door where Lemone, Captain Brock, Mrs Speckle and Kite were waiting in the hallway. Pickle's loss had been felt keenly, not just by Wilma, but by everyone at Clarissa Cottage and those around them, so they were all there now to pay their last respects.

'Come and hold my hand, Wilma,' said Kite, reaching out. 'You stay close to me. I won't leave you.'

Wilma let her hand fall into Kite's and watched as Inspector Lemone helped lift Pickle's coffin from the table. As the coffin went past her, Wilma felt her heart breaking and she leaned into Kite, who squeezed her hand a little more tightly.

The early morning sun was beautiful, the sky, a glorious, gentle pink, and as the coffin was carried slowly and respectfully to the grave Wilma could hear the sweet calls of the dawn chorus. It was as if the birds of Cooper had come to sing Pickle off. They gathered around the hole that had been dug in preparation as Mr Goodman and Lemone carefully lowered Pickle's coffin into its final resting place.

Theodore, hands clasped before him, cleared his throat. 'I think it's appropriate that I say a few words before we say goodbye to Pickle. I don't think any of us will ever forget him. His bravery, his fortitude, his love for Wilma, all these things were testament to his fine character. He wasn't *always* well behaved,' Theodore added, with a gentle smile. 'I think we've all lost a few corn crumbles to him . . .'

'He ate a whole plateful once!' said Kite, putting her arm round Wilma's shoulders.

'And a pie! And a roast leg of lamb!' added Mrs Speckle.

'Dog after my own heart,' said Lemone, reaching for his handkerchief.

Wilma mustered a small smile, in spite of herself.

Theodore looked down at her, his eyes filled with kindness. 'Our dear Pickle – rest in peace,' he said, taking a handful of soil and throwing it gently on to the coffin.

Wilma watched as everyone else took turns to scatter earth on top of the coffin. Then, helped by Mrs Speckle and Kite, Wilma came forward and reached down to gather a handful of dirt. She held it out over the grave and let it fall, hearing the gentle thud against the coffin.

'Goodbye, Pickle,' she whispered. 'And thank you.'

And so, reader, let us draw a gentle curtain over Wilma's grief. Our darling Pickle has gone to chase rabbits in the sky. Happy travels, little beagle. Happy travels.

Chapter 25

If there was one thing Wilma was sure about, it was not letting her beloved dog down. He had devoted his short life to being brave and doing the right thing and now, with the island in turmoil, it was more important than ever to tread a steadfast path and not give up.

As the days passed, Wilma began to feel a little better and although she would carry the sadness of her loss for a long while yet, she knew that there were things to be done – things Pickle would have wanted done. There were great problems to surmount on the island of Cooper. Theodore P. Goodman was no longer a detective and Barbu had the island in the grip of terror. Citizens were under curfew, Criminal Elements were ransacking houses and everyone lived in fear.

A week after Pickle's death, when Theodore felt that Wilma was strong enough again, he called a secret meeting at Clarissa

Cottage, inviting not just Captain Brock, Lemone, Mrs Speckle and Kite, but also Glenda Blaize and the Keeper of Cooper Law, Melba Toest. He'd also invited someone that everyone else was a little more than surprised to see . . .

'What's she doing here?' blustered Glenda, on seeing her disgraced sister, Brenda, sitting by the fire. 'She's the reason we're in this mess.'

'I can't apologize enough,' said Brenda, standing and pacing. 'I've been an A-grade fool. But, please, I beg of you all, give me the chance to try to put things right. I know I can be of use.'

'Everyone deserves a second chance,' explained Theodore, taking a small puff on his pipe. 'I think it's a fair assessment that she was blinded by love and ideology.'

'Hmph. Well. Things couldn't be worse,' said Glenda, taking out a cigar and lighting it. 'And the most awful part of it is that I can't see a single way round any of it. Melba here says the fellow has us fair and square. Cooper laws simply don't cover this eventuality. It's madness.'

'We can't give up though,' said Wilma, passing round a plate of corn crumbles. 'We'll never give up.'

'Of course we won't,' agreed Theodore, just missing out on a biscuit as Lemone took the last two on the plate. 'If we do, then Barbu D'Anvers will destroy this island. And we can't stand idly by and let that happen.'

223

'Is there anything wonky in Cooper Law?' asked Wilma, turning to Melba Toest, who was poring over an enormous book of by-laws. 'You know, a bit sideways and unexpected?'

'Well,' began Melba, pinching the top of her nose, 'there is something. But it's a long shot. If it can be proved that the incumbent Cooperate General is currently breaking a law, then we might be able to do something about it. Breaking laws in the past doesn't count. He has to be breaking a law right now. Which is going to be near impossible to prove as he's declared stealing to be perfectly legal. It has to be something else.'

'Can't we just go to Rascal Rock and catch him at something else?' suggested Wilma excitedly. 'I'm sure it won't be hard. There's plenty of criminal activities other than stealing and he's bound to be doing at least one of them.'

'But how on earth can we get in there and find out?' asked Captain Brock. 'The place is crawling with Criminal Elements and we're vastly outnumbered.'

'We can go down the manhole,' explained Wilma, the light returning to her eyes. 'The one I found before the Final Naming Ceremony. Where me and Pickle . . .' Wilma paused and took a deep breath. This was no time to get emotional. 'Anyway, that manhole leads right into the heart of his lair.'

'Excellent thinking, Wilma,' said Theodore encouragingly.

'But we've got another problem,' said Melba. Everyone

turned and looked at her. 'Cooper Law states that only a detective can unseat a Cooperate General. Mr Goodman has been sacked. Cooper Island no longer has a detective.'

'Yes, we do,' said Theodore, grabbing his coat. 'We have Wilma.'

Wilma blinked. 'But I'm only an apprentice!' she yelled as she ran after her mentor.

'Not for long you're not!' said Theodore, with a smile.

Wilma stared up at her headmistress, Kite Lambard. The others stood quietly in a semi-circle around them, the mood sombre and critical. In Kite's hand was a thin blue book. 'Are you ready?' Kite asked, resting a hand on Wilma's shoulder. The young apprentice nodded. This was a momentous occasion.

'Wilma Tenderfoot,' began Kite, 'place your hand on the Academy textbook. Do you promise to defend the weak, the unfortunate and the set-upon, and to fight for truth and justice?'

Wilma gulped. 'I do promise. Cross my heart.'

Kite nodded towards Theodore, who stepped forward with a rectangular red box in his hand. Opening it, he took out a golden badge and handed it to Kite. 'Then I have great pleasure in declaring you junior detective, first class.' She leaned forward and pinned it on to Wilma's pinafore strap.

'Oh my,' said Wilma, a little overwhelmed. 'I'm actually a

detective. I can't believe it. Is it really true, Mr Goodman?'

'Yes it is, Wilma,' said Theodore, reaching for something else in the box. 'And, because you're now a proper detective, you get one of these.'

He lifted out a gleaming magnifying glass: gold-rimmed with a soft leather handle.

Wilma gasped. 'It's just like your one, Mr Goodman! I've never had anything so precious in my life.' At its base there was a small clasp, and using this she clipped it to the Clue Ring on her pinafore belt with considerable pride.

'Take good care of it, Wilma,' added Theodore, with a twitch of his moustache. 'It will help you in many a scrape. Have no doubt of that.'

Wilma stared down at the badge on her strap and the magnifying glass at her belt. The burden of responsibility hung heavy. All of Cooper was now reliant on her, but a moment of doubt shot through her. Was she up to the task?

Theodore, noticing Wilma's wavering, took the initiative. 'Congratulations, Detective Tenderfoot,' he said, shaking her hand. 'I expect you're feeling a little anxious, nervous even. But there's no need. I can't think of anyone I'd rather rely on. You're in charge now, but all of us are here to help you. We're a team. Isn't that right, everyone?'

The others crowded round, patting Wilma on the back

and making encouraging noises.

'Couldn't be more pleased,' said Inspector Lemone, beaming. 'You'll be magnificent.'

Wilma mustered a weak smile. 'Thank you, everyone. I know that this is the most massive responsibility I've ever been given. I can't pretend that I know what I'm doing. Because I don't. But I will try to do my best.'

'Right then, Detective Tenderfoot, are you ready to lead us to Rascal Rock?' asked Theodore proudly.

'Yes, Mr Goodman, I am,' said Wilma. 'The entrance to the tunnel I went down was a manhole in Measly Down. Though I wouldn't even be half surprised if most of the manholes on Cooper led to tunnels.'

'Wait a moment,' said Theodore, with a steady voice. 'I don't think it's such a good idea for so large a group to all go together. We're too conspicuous.'

'Oh yes,' said Wilma, spinning on the spot. 'I remember that word. It means really noticeable which is never good when you're creeping and sneaking.'

'Might I suggest, if you don't mind, Wilma,' asked Theodore, 'that we also consider a diversion? So that any creeping and sneaking goes even more unnoticed.'

'Yes! What he said,' cried Wilma excitedly, pointing at Theodore and nodding furiously. 'I know! How's this. Why

227

don't we split into two? We can have the Creep Team. And the Diversion Team. So the Creep Team will be me, Mr Goodman, Inspector Lemone and Miss Lambard. And the Diversion Team will be Captain Brock and his men, Miss Toest and Glenda and Brenda Blaize?'

Everyone in the room looked at each other and nodded.

'The Creep Team will go with me down the manhole,' said Wilma.

'And, if you like, Wilma,' said Captain Brock, stepping forward, 'I could lead the Diversion Team to Rascal Rock above ground. We could go in the 2nd Hawks Brigade cart. And once we get there we can keep the Criminal Elements busy while you do your investigating.'

'Melba and I could pretend we have extensive post-ceremonial paperwork for Barbu to sign?' chipped in Glenda.

'And I could just go as someone to be shouted at,' suggested Brenda, looking hopeful. 'Every troop needs one of those. I think it's a moral-support thing.'

'And I'm coming too! On the creep team,' cried Mrs Speckle, swinging a rolling pin into a knitted holster on her hip. 'Think of me as the muscle of the outfit.'

'Well, that's all settled then,' said Wilma, her eyes gleaming. 'So does everyone know what they're doing?'

'We do!' they all cried.

'Then onward to Rascal Rock!' yelled Wilma, thrusting a finger into the air.

'To Rascal Rock!' they all yelled in response.

This is the point in a film where you'd hear stirring music that might make you want to jump out of your seat, punch the air and shout, 'COME ON!'

The fight back starts HERE, reader. Get on board.

Chapter 26

Dusk was falling and, with storm clouds gathering again to the east, a chill wind had sprung up. Wilma, wrapped in her duffel coat, led the team through the back alleys from Clarissa Cottage. Even though she knew the pathways like the back of her hand, the journey felt perilous, as if, at any moment, some terrible fate might befall them and, with that in mind, she led her team with caution. Things on Cooper weren't the same since Barbu had come to power. The vast majority of Farsiders and Lowsiders alike had locked themselves inside, so terrified were they of being robbed by the gangs of Criminal Elements who were running amok, high on squifty juice, celebrating their evil master's seizure of the island.

As the team neared Measly Down, they could hear raucous noises carrying on the wind. An undercurrent of jeering and drunken singing was peppered with sounds of glass shattering and the crashing of chairs and tables being broken up to make fires. To get to the manhole, they had to cross the square directly in front of the Great Gate, but ahead of them Wilma could see smoke and men fighting. Deciding they needed to stop and think about what to do for the best, Wilma ducked into a dark culvert and gestured to the others to follow her.

'It's an absolute disgrace,' said Glenda, leaning her head out from the alley to watch the chaos. 'Only a week that man's been in charge and look at the place. They've torn down the flagpole! The statue of Old Jacquis and the Porpoise has been toppled and there's a man up there wearing the Cooper flag as a pair of pants! I can barely believe my eyes.'

'I'm not sure how we're going to get across without being noticed,' said Wilma, gulping. 'And I can't lie, Mr Goodman, I'm a little bit afraid. When I say *little bit*, I mean quite a lot. And I'm not sure what to do.'

Theodore put a steadying hand on the junior detective's shoulder. 'The situation is serious, Wilma,' he said, his moustache twitching. 'And being afraid is perfectly normal. But fear is a detective's friend. It means we are alert to danger. We have one advantage. The Criminal Elements have clearly been enjoying several barrels of squifty juice, which means their minds won't be as sharp as they otherwise might be.'

Captain Brock was using his exceptional looking skills to

scan the top of the alley. 'There are sentries on corners, four in all, and more Criminal Elements posted on rooftops. I can see six. There's one man with a telescope and behind him fifteen men with clubs. And I don't want to alarm anyone, but there are now seven sentries in position behind us. We're surrounded.'

'We'll never get to the manhole without being spotted,' said Brenda Blaize, frowning.

Theodore looked at Wilma with a sense of urgency. 'What have you learned at the Academy and in your training with me that might be relevant now? Try to think.'

Wilma's entire face was screwed up into a tight ball of concentration as she racked her brains for an answer. 'I know, Mr Goodman,' she said suddenly, as a cunning plan popped into her head. 'We need to try to blend in so we don't get noticed. Which means we should all pretend to be sizzled out of our minds on squifty juice! So instead of creeping we should just make loads of noise and stumble around a bit. That way we won't look out of place.'

Theodore smiled. 'Very good, Wilma,' he said, with a proud chuckle. 'Very good.'

'Right then,' said Wilma, excited by her plan. 'Everybody ready?'

Everyone nodded. Mrs Speckle undid the top button of her roll-neck cardigan. 'So I look dishevelled,' she explained to

Inspector Lemone, who promptly undid his too. Captain Brock set his cap at an angle, Glenda and Brenda messed up their hair and draped their arms about each other, Melba smeared some dribble over her chin, Theodore bent down and rubbed some mud on his face and Kite practised her best cross-eyed look and pretended to have hiccups.

'I saw Madam Skratch from the Institute for Woeful Children a bit worse for wear once. She bumped into furniture and pointed at things a lot. So I'll copy that,' said Wilma, taking her arms out of her duffel coat and leaving it hanging from her head by the hood. 'And shout a lot. And then maybe cry. OK. Let's go!'

Leading the gang out from the culvert Wilma, noticing a Criminal Element at the top of the alley turning to look at her, instantly shouted something insensible and walked sideways into a bin. Bouncing off it, she then held her arms in the air and, tottering unsteadily, threw her head back and roared 'ARRGGGGGGGH!' as loud as she could.

Behind her, Theodore and Kite were shoving each other, Captain Brock was crawling on his hands and knees while Glenda and Brenda staggered forward, stopping every now and again to pretend to retch. Inspector Lemone peered out from behind the corner of the culvert and gulped. He had no acting skills to rely on. A short, sudden stab of panic coursed through him.

How was he going to ham it up to the other side of the square? Mrs Speckle was already waddling away up the alley, one of her knitted wellington boots half off her foot. He couldn't let her down.

'Come on, Lemone,' he whispered to himself, 'you can do this!' And, legs trembling, he stepped out from the shadows, looking anxiously about him as he went.

Just then, a lumpy-looking man with wild eyes and gravestone teeth veered lecherously over to Mrs Speckle, grabbed her by the shoulders and without a whisker of warning planted a fat wet kiss on her lips.

'Ohhhhhhhhhhhhhh!' wailed Mrs Speckle, pushing the brute off, but just as she was about to give him a sharp piece of her mind, a fist came flying in, landing on the fellow's chin. With a roll of his eyes, the assailant fell to the floor. Mrs Speckle, pushing up her double-bobble hats, turned to see who had saved her.

'Not having that,' said Inspector Lemone, rubbing his knuckles angrily.

Mrs Speckle, who was a woman not naturally given to softer moments, raised an eyebrow. 'Well, Inspector Lemone,' she said, with a small smile, 'fancy you coming to my rescue. You can take my arm, if you like. See me safely to the manhole.'

Inspector Lemone swallowed and stared at the object of his

affection for all these years. He still couldn't believe she even knew his name and here she was, proffering her arm and asking to be escorted. This was, without a doubt, the finest moment of Lemone's life to date.

'Well done, Wilma,' said Theodore quietly, as they all made it one by one to the other side of the square. 'Capital plan. And expertly executed. You're doing very well.'

Wilma beamed. It was a proud moment. But she wasn't going to rest on her laurels.

With the manhole cover now lifted off, Wilma gave a grave nod. 'Right then. I guess this is it,' she said. 'Hopefully we'll see you all again later, diversion team. But for the rest of us . . . down and on!'

'Am I going to fit?' asked Lemone quietly, as Wilma leaped down into the hole.

'Don't worry,' said Mrs Speckle, rubbing his forearm. 'I'll just stamp on your shoulders till you shove through.'

Ahhh. Ain't love grand?

Pssst. It's exciting, isn't it?

235

Chapter 27

Wilma searched the length of the dingily lit tunnel.

Behind her, Theodore and Kite were tugging on Lemone's legs, dangling from the hole above, as Mrs Speckle hissed, 'One more shove and he'll be through!' and with a mighty grunt Lemone popped downward.

'Never understand why they make those things so narrow,' he panted, standing up and dusting himself down.

'Right,' said Wilma. 'When I was here with Pickle . . .' She stopped, her voice sticking in her throat. Being in the tunnel brought the memory of that terrible moment flooding back. Not only that, but before long she would be facing Pickle's killer once more. For a moment, she wondered if she could go on. She pressed her eyes tight shut, took a deep breath and reopened them. She had to do this. For Pickle. 'We don't want to run into Barbu just yet,' she said, quietly. 'We need to find some evidence against him. Espionage is the key. So let's not go the way I did before. That tunnel came out in his quarters. There's a junction up ahead. It goes to the right. We'll see where that leads instead.'

'Good thinking, Wilma,' whispered Theodore as Wilma, keeping to the edges of the tunnel, led her friends onward.

When they reached the junction, Wilma held a hand up and very slowly poked her head round the corner so she could squint down the tunnel. She could see the warm glow of a fire in the distance.

'There, look,' she whispered to the others. 'That must be a guard. Wonder what he's guarding? Hopefully some sort of criminal activity. How are we going to get past?'

'We'll have to divert his attention,' replied Theodore.

Wilma looked back towards the fire. She could just make out the shadow of a burly-looking figure picking his nose.

'I bet he's been down here ages,' she whispered. 'Which means he's probably hungry. Has anyone got any food on them?'

Theodore, Kite and Mrs Speckle all shook their heads and then turned to Inspector Lemone, who was looking distinctly uncomfortable.

'I've got corn crumbles in my pocket. But you can't possibly be suggesting that I . . .'

'Hand them over, Lemone,' whispered Theodore, giving his

friend a soothing pat on the arm. 'It's a noble sacrifice.'

Inspector Lemone blinked. 'But Mrs Speckle made them . . .' he said weakly. 'And they're corn crumbles. Corn crumbles.' He stopped, his voice catching in his throat, but he knew he had no choice. With a devastated sigh, he reached into his pocket and pulled out what he had.

'Thanks,' said Wilma, taking them. 'Now we just need to throw them, but I don't think I can chuck that far.'

'Hang on. I've got a catapult in my satchel,' whispered Kite, eyes widening. 'I've been carrying it around for years. Crumbs. I've been useful at last. Amazing.'

Wilma took the catapult and placed one of the biscuits in its pouch.

'Try to aim beyond the fire,' advised Theodore, 'so that he turns away from us. That way we can creep past him into the side tunnel to the right.'

Wilma closed one eye and stuck her tongue out in concentration. Pulling the elastic as far back as she could, she let go, but her aim was off and the first corn crumble biscuit hit the ceiling, disintegrating on contact. Inspector Lemone bit his lip. What senseless waste. Wilma shook her head and placed the second biscuit into the catapult.

'Bit lower,' whispered Theodore, pointing with his finger, 'towards the fire.'

Again, Wilma twanged the elastic and let the biscuit fly, but, as luck would have it, it landed slap bang in the middle of the burning barrel, and they watched in slight horror as a small flame shot upward and the biscuit incinerated on the spot. Inspector Lemone gulped. This was AWFUL.

'Last chance,' she mumbled, determined to get it right. 'This is the one.'

Catapulting their final corn crumble, Wilma, heart in her mouth, watched as the biscuit flew silently through the air, over the top of the glowing barrel, to land gently with a skidding bounce on the floor beyond.

She'd done it!

The thug manning the post turned and sniffed the air. 'Wassat?' he grunted, scanning the floor. 'Oooooh, biscuit . . .'

He bent down to enjoy his quarry, closing his eyes in delight, and Wilma and the others slipped silently past him.

'That's peculiar,' whispered Kite, as they came to the end of the passageway. 'It's a dead end. Why would Barbu have someone guarding a dead end?'

Wilma stared up at the wall in front of them. Kite was right. It *was* peculiar. The walls to the side of the passageway were made from stone, but the wall at the end seemed to be a slightly different colour and texture. Wilma lay her hand against it and then, clenching her fingers into a fist, she rapped gently against

239

it. There was a dullness to the thud.

Theodore, realizing what she was thinking, encouraged her. 'Rap gently from left to right, Wilma,' he said. 'I think you might be on to something.'

She tapped again. *Thud. Thud.* And then, suddenly, the noise changed. A lighter, sharper noise sounded. She struck again. There was no doubt about it – there was a section of the wall that was hollow.

'I think this bit is wood,' said Wilma, excited by her find. 'Of course! It's a secret passageway. We were going to do them in our Academy lessons, Miss Lambard. Can you remember what the Academy handbook said about them?'

'Ooh,' said Kite, eyes widening at being put on the spot. 'Well . . . the thing is . . .'

'Step aside,' said Mrs Speckle, shoving her cardigan up to her elbows. 'Leave this to me.'

And before anyone could say another word Mrs Speckle lowered herself into a crouch and, without warning, leaped into the air, spun round at speed and with one leg extended broke through the wood with ease.

'I am trained in kung fu,' she explained, with a sniff as she landed. 'Well, come on. Don't just stand there gawping.' And, with that, she disappeared through the shattered wood.

And what this should teach you, children, is that women are

mysterious creatures capable of a multitude of hidden talents. So don't forget it.

Behind the secret panel was a stone staircase with a heavy wooden door at the top.

Wilma leaned her ear against the door. 'I can't hear anything,' she whispered.

As quietly as she could, Wilma turned the doorknob until she heard an almost imperceptible click of the bolting mechanism as it retracted from the lock. Gingerly she pushed the door into the room beyond and poked her head through the crack. It led into a long corridor that was painted a dull green, not unlike a churned sea on a winter's day. Giving a glance in both directions and realizing the coast was clear, she stepped through, gesturing to the others to follow her.

'Which way now?' asked Mrs Speckle.

Suddenly they heard banging and crashing coming from behind a swing door on the left up ahead. Steam was pouring out from the bottom of it and an almost over-bearing smell of boiling cabbage filled the air.

'That must be the kitchen,' whispered Wilma, pointing in its direction. 'Maybe it's Mrs Scrabs? Barbu's housekeeper?'

'Mrs Scrabs?' said Mrs Speckle, shoving up her bobble hats. 'Sally Scrabs. Dreadful woman. Thin as a whippet and as sour as a lemon. Wouldn't trust her as far as I could throw

241

her. Tiny eyes. Always spells trouble.'

'Mrs Scrabs is skinny?' said Wilma with surprise. 'I pictured her as a big fat lady, given the size of the food delivery that was going in while Barbu was still away.'

'Regardless of her size, what was she doing here anyway? Taking large food deliveries when Barbu was banished?' said Theodore, his moustache twitching.

'Do you think it might be something connected to a criminal activity, Mr Goodman?' whispered Wilma, her eyes flashing. 'If she's scrawnier than a stick, then where was all the food going?'

'Or to whom,' said Theodore, exchanging an excited look with Kite.

'You don't think . . .' answered the headmistress, raising a hand to her mouth.

But Mrs Speckle was already moving towards the kitchen and the others suddenly had to rush to catch up with her.

'Stand aside,' said Mrs Speckle, through gritted teeth. 'I've waited a long time for this.'

Like a bullet from a gun, Mrs Speckle shot into the kitchen, arms outstretched. Mrs Scrabs, startled at the intrusion, went to let out a scream, but before she could do so Mrs Speckle reached for a lump of dough and threw it straight into the housekeeper's mouth, plugging her cries instantly. Mrs Scrabs instantly fell backwards and Mrs Speckle snatched her up by the scruff of the neck, dragging her to the floor.

'Mrs Speckle is a SENSATION,' declared Wilma, mouth agape.

NEVER underestimate a middle-aged woman with a rolling pin. NEVER.

By the way . . . who do YOU think all that food was for?

Chapter 28

Trevor was having a terrible week. First, the Great Gate had been closed and now, having been forced open again by the Lowsider uprising, his beloved border booth was overrun with Criminal Elements.

'No,' he shouted, grabbing an ink pad from a small bald woman with an enormous nose, 'that's not for public use. That's Official Border Equipment.'

A wooden hand came out from a hole in the wall and slapped him round the face.

'Get out!' he yelled, exasperated. 'Criminal Elements are not allowed in the Peeper Cupboard! You've got NO respect!'

'Official delegation to see Mr D'Anvers,' said a voice, coming from the booth window.

Trevor swivelled round in his chair to see Captain Brock

and his team and, standing just over his shoulder, Melba, Glenda and Brenda.

Trevor blinked. His booth was in chaos.

'Sorry, it's been pandemonium this evening. Official delegation you say? And you are?'

'Captain Brock, 2nd Hawks Brigade. And I have with me Glenda Blaize, the former Cooperate General; Melba Toest, Keeper of Cooper Law; and Brenda Blaize. They will be assisting Mr D'Anvers in some personal matters. The orange questionnaire you might want to give us is folded and is to be found beneath the wooden tray of paperclips. We are in something of a rush so perhaps we could forgo the completion of the pink procedural paper, which, at the current moment, is tucked sideways into a magazine on the second shelf to your left. In fact, we are in such a rush that we'd be grateful if you could waive all form-filling and just stamp us in.'

Trevor stared up with incredulity, his mouth hanging open. 'But . . .' he began.

'The stamp is sitting in the mug in front of you. It has tea on it. You may want to wipe it.'

In something of a stupor, Trevor reached into the mug and pulled out a small red ink stamp.

'The ink pad is in your top pocket,' pointed out Captain Brock, with authority.

'So it is,' mumbled Trevor, in a daze. 'Just stamp you in, you say . . . Well . . . it's highly irregular but . . .'

'Four stamps, please. Lickety-split.'

Trevor gulped, grabbed a random piece of paper, stamped it four times and handed it over. All his professional pride had vanished.

'Access to the Lowside granted,' he said feebly. As Captain Brock saluted him, Trevor tried to salute back. But he'd forgotten to let go of his mug and, as he raised his hand, he hit himself on the forehead, sending cold tea dripping down his face.

It really had been a *terrible* week.

Captain Brock drove the Hawks Brigade cart at speed through the crowds of Criminal Elements still gathered near the gate on the Lowside. They were standing round fires, cooking pigeons on spits and toasting their newfound fortune. As Captain Brock and his team passed them by, it seemed for a moment as if the group might make their passage without incident, but then suddenly a large, hairy, thuggish-looking type stepped into their path. His partners in crime were quick to join him.

Captain Brock slowed the horses and the thug yelled, 'Hang on! Ain't you the old Hawks Brigade and Cooperate General? What business you got here? We should give you a tumble! Learn you some lessons.'

'No need for that, I'm sure,' said Glenda confidently. 'We're on our way to see Barbu D'Anvers. At his request. I'm sure he wouldn't like to hear of us being treated badly before we got there.'

'On the contrary,' said a short, sneering, scar-faced rogue, edging closer, 'I think Mr D'Anvers would want you roughed up a little.'

Captain Brock looked about him quickly. They needed to get away, and fast. But they were surrounded. The crowd of villains was snarling now and edging closer, and one of them was reaching for a dagger. Melba gasped as she saw the blade flash in the firelight.

Brenda, thinking fast, reached into her satchel and pulled out one of her unused bombs. As she threw it down at the feet of the approaching scoundrels, a huge plume of smoke gushed up and outward into the faces of their assailants, making them cough and splutter.

Without a moment's hesitation, Captain Brock gave a sharp crack of the whip, and they were away once more.

Captain Brock pulled the pony up just short of Um Bridge. Below them, over the edge of the cliff tops, the wind was causing the sea to swell, sending powerful waves crashing against the granite of Rascal Rock. The air was thick with the smell of sea salt, and above them the bare branches of a willow tree whipped and thrashed as the low, dread moan of the gathering storm ebbed and swelled. Captain Brock leaped from the buggy, frock coat flapping in the wind, and stared towards Barbu's lair.

'I see ten men,' shouted Captain Brock over the gale. 'Far side of the bridge. Six men around the turret. And someones or somethings hanging from a pole at the bridge entrance. We're severely outnumbered.' He turned, his face filled with concern. 'What we are about to do is extremely dangerous, but rest assured, ladies, if needs be, I'll protect you till my dying breath.'

'And we you, Captain Brock,' replied Glenda Blaize, her eyes steely with resolve. 'Your bravery is never in question. But we're a team, and you mustn't feel that because we are women you bear the burden of responsibility. Do not imagine that as the more delicate sex we do not possess robust intentions. If needs dictate that I must fight, then fight I will.'

'Me too,' echoed Melba, clutching her files close to her chest.

'And I,' said Brenda, stepping forward. 'Though I think I'd better go in disguise, under the circumstances.' And she pulled a wig of pink frizzy hair that she'd brought along for that very reason on to her head.

'Courage is being prepared to stand up and be counted,'

continued Glenda, the wind blowing through her hair. 'The welfare of this island is a cause for which I am happy to die.'

Captain Brock nodded, his chest filled with emotion. 'It is an honour and a privilege to stand with you ladies. A finer regiment I have never known.' He threw back his shoulders and saluted.

'Then let it begin,' cried Glenda. 'Onward!'

Brenda stopped in her tracks and stared up at the pole by the bridge entrance. 'Are you all right?' she asked, with some unease.

Gerald Mothma stared down at her, looking desperately uncomfortable. 'Not really,' he answered. 'I've been hanging by my pants for the last week. If you could get me down, I'd be very grateful.'

'Gosh,' answered Brenda, her eyes popping wide. 'Absolutely. What's the best way? Pull your pants down? Or pull your pants up?'

Glenda quickly stepped forward, stopping Brenda from helping Gerald.

'Actually,' she said, her face grave and apologetic, 'I'm very sorry. We're on an undercover mission to save the island.' She looked up at Gerald. 'And if we let you down it'll rather give the game away. I hope you understand.'

Gerald gulped bravely and nodded. 'Righty-ho. Not to worry,' he replied, trying a smile. 'Any chance you could pass me up the lump of cheese from my lunchbox down there? I'm frightfully hungry.'

Suddenly, 'HOLD THERE!' yelled a thick-necked man pointing a rifle squarely towards Captain Brock and his extended team. 'What's your business?'

Melba, sensing this was her moment, stepped out from behind the Blaize sisters.

'I am the Keeper of Cooper Law,' she explained, reaching for the forged document she had made. 'And we are the official delegation come to see Mr D'Anvers at his request.' She flapped the paper sharply in front of the thug's nose.

'Give me that,' he growled, snatching the end of it. Nine men were standing behind him and they all crowded round to take a good look at it.

'Can anyone actually read?' Melba heard one of them whisper. There were some low, dismissive grunts. 'Looks proper enough. Got a swirly thing up there. Inky thing down there. What's that?'

'Dragon?' suggested one of them, scratching his head.

'I heard dragons are totally official,' mumbled another. 'I think the dragon means it's real.'

'Are you sure?' asked the thick-set man. 'I thought that was

250

unicorns? Right, show of hands. Who thinks the dragon thing makes it proper?'

They all stuck their hands up.

'Yes,' declared the man, turning back to Melba. 'That all seems above board. On you go. Mr D'Anvers is down the corridor, third door on the left.'

'We're in,' whispered Brenda, her heart thumping. 'We're in!'

Creep Team downstairs with Mrs Scrabs, Diversion Team upstairs with Barbu D'Anvers. Can it get ANY MORE THRILLING? (The answer is YES.)

Chapter 29

'So these new shoes make me how tall?' asked Barbu, staring at himself in a floor-to-ceiling mirror.

'Five-and-twenty spans, sir,' said a wiry-looking tailor with half-moon spectacles, who was standing on a box, holding a measuring tape.

'And how tall am I now? When I put my crown on?' Barbu bent at the knees so that he could put his head inside a giant crown that was resting on a stand. Very carefully, he stood up, lifting the enormous coronet into the air.

'Hang on, sir,' said the tailor. 'I'll just fetch a bigger ladder.' A wooden ladder was wheeled into position and the tailor scurried to the top of it, dropping his measuring tape downward. 'Well! Mr D'Anvers! You're now taller than my tape. So that's thirty spans and a bit extra.'

'Thirty spans and a bit extra . . .' smirked Barbu smugly.

'What does that make me as tall as? Janty, consult the book!'

The young apprentice flicked through a book entitled *What is as tall as you?*.

'According to this,' he replied, 'you're now as tall as a pear tree, a significant outhouse or half a lighthouse.'

'Half a lighthouse!' declared the villain, his eyes blazing with delight.

'But without the shoes and crown,' Janty continued, flicking backwards, 'you're as high as a picket fence. A really small one. That's what the book says. Really small.'

Barbu's look of delight turned to one of rage. 'Have you forgotten the law I passed just moments ago, Janty? The word *SMALL* has been banned! Eradicated from usage! It no longer exists! You really are becoming the most grand irritant. Are you STILL moping about that stupid dog?'

Janty tossed the book to one side and stood defiant before his master. 'You didn't have to kill him.'

'Oh GOD, how many times do we have to go through this?' said Barbu, teetering across the room towards an ermine-draped throne. 'I wasn't even aiming for the wretched dog. I was trying to kill that annoying girl! Who, I might add, I would have dispatched if you hadn't grabbed me by the arm in . . . what – a moment of madness? So it's your fault that dog is dead. Not mine. Do you know . . . I think I've had enough of you. All you do is scuff about looking shabby and being grumpy. I don't even like you. You've outlived your usefulness, just like your father. Toss him out, someone! I'm done with him.' Barbu waved a dismissive hand in the boy's direction.

Two guards, who had been sitting playing cards in the corner, started towards Janty, but the boy strode fearlessly over to Barbu's throne.

'How dare you speak about my father like that!' he yelled. 'He was a greater man than you will ever be!'

Barbu stared, incredulous. 'I'm sorry? Oh no. I fear you are much mistaken. Your father was weak and pointless. I would have killed him that night I went to his workshop to question him, but I was beaten to it by that curator's annoying blow dart. Unfortunately.' Barbu's lip curled into a triumphant and evil smile.

Janty felt a burning hatred surge in his chest. His hands tightened into fists and a red mist descended. He launched himself at the diminutive villain, but just as he was about to land a punch he felt a hand grabbing him from behind, yanking him backwards. It was Tully.

'Get out of here,' the henchman muttered in his ear, as he dragged the boy out into the corridor. 'Or he'll kill you. Go on, run!' Tully turned and slammed the door in Janty's face.

There were several people in the corridor. It was Captain Brock, his team and the ladies, waiting to go in and see Barbu. Raging inside, Janty pushed rudely past them, but as he did so he overheard Melba whisper to Glenda, 'I hope Wilma and the others are all right . . .'

Janty stopped and watched as the group entered the throne room, his mind racing. Was Wilma inside Rascal Rock? And, if she was, what was she doing? And why was Captain Brock here? Something was afoot. And he wanted to know what.

'Oh, what is all this?' groaned Barbu, seeing the official delegation being ushered in. 'I'm in charge now. That means I don't have to be bothered with anything. I rule. So go away.'

'It's just one last formality, Cooperate D'Anvers,' said Melba, stepping forward. 'A few forms to sign and then that's it. Once it's done you will never have to be troubled by us again.'

Barbu scowled and then, seeing Glenda, curled his lip and said, 'What's old leather-face doing here? She's been sacked, hasn't she?'

'I have to sign over some important Cooper buildings to you,' she explained. 'It means you get more stuff.'

'More stuff, you say?' said Barbu, with a little more interest. 'Oh, all right then. Let's get this over with. What do I have to sign?'

Melba stepped forward and thumped a huge pile of documents in front of the villain.

'OH, YOU HAVE GOT TO BE JOKING!' he screamed, totally obscured by the papers.

'I'm afraid not, Cooperate D'Anvers,' replied Melba sweetly. 'Until you sign every single paper, you're not officially in charge of anything.'

Barbu grunted and held out his hand. 'PEN!' he yelled.

I don't want you to get your hopes up, reader, but part one of the plan appears to be working . . .

Chapter 30

Wilma ducked as a large rolling pin smashed through the kitchen-door window above her. The battle in the kitchen was now at full pelt and Mrs Scrabs, who had come round and was fighting back royally, had leaped on top of the stove and was about to pounce on Mrs Speckle's shoulders.

'Mrs Scrabs has now jumped!' said Wilma, commentating for the others. 'Oh dear – she's got Mrs Speckle pinned down on the chopping board. Oh. Wait. Mrs Speckle's pushed her off. She's got Mrs Scrabs by the neck and the pants. She's lifting her above her head. She's spinning her round. And now she's thrown her into the fridge . . .'

'Do you think I should . . . you know . . .' began Inspector Lemone, straightening his tie, 'go in and help?'

'I suspect you'd be more of a hindrance,' replied Theodore, peeking over the top of Wilma's head.

The kitchen air was filled with flour. Mrs Speckle was covered in broken eggs and custard and Mrs Scrabs was fumbling about on the floor for a pack of butter. Finding it, she unwrapped it and threw it with vigour towards Mrs Speckle, hitting her in the eye. Momentarily blinded, Mrs Speckle floundered and Mrs Scrabs saw her opportunity. She climbed up a rack of meats and, after flying through the air, landed face down on top of Mrs Speckle.

Wilma winced. 'Ouch!' she said, letting out a thin whistle. 'Powerslam. Mrs Speckle is dazed. But wait — she's flipped round . . . she's got Mrs Scrabs by the ankle. And Mrs Scrabs is DOWN. Mrs Speckle's got her in a face-buster. Oh! And now it's a double-leg takedown from Mrs Scrabs. She's trying to set up the ankle lock! Mrs Speckle's in the Boston crab! Surely there can be no getting out of this! But wait! Mrs Speckle's kicked Mrs Scrabs off and into the bins! Is she going for the choke-slam? She is! It's a masterly move! And Mrs Scrabs is back down again! Can Mrs Speckle finish this with a power-bomb? She's lifting Mrs Scrabs above her head! And down she goes! There's no coming back from that! She's a-one! She's a-two! And she's a-three. It's all over for the housekeeper from Rascal Rock!'

'Stand back, Wilma,' advised Theodore, as he entered the decimated kitchen, the others following cautiously behind.

Spitting a bit of eggshell from her mouth, Mrs Speckle, still

panting, looked up. 'She still won't tell me what she or Barbu have been up to. Want me to use the cheese grater?'

'No,' replied Theodore quickly, 'I don't think that will be—'

'I can help you,' said a voice behind them. They all turned to see a slightly red-cheeked Janty looking bashfully at them.

Inspector Lemone narrowed his eyes. 'Sneaking about as usual! Well, I shan't let you run back and snitch! You've caused enough trouble!'

'No,' cried Janty, protesting. 'Please. I want to help.'

'Give the boy a chance,' Theodore intervened. 'After all, for all the bad he's done, he also let Wilma get away in the tunnels, didn't you, boy?'

Janty flushed even more. He hadn't known if Wilma would tell anyone that. Wilma snuck him a small smile.

'What do you know?' Mr Goodman went on, meeting Janty's desperate gaze.

'Not much,' said the boy, still held tightly by Inspector Lemone. 'But I did follow Mrs Scrabs the other day. She was taking food on a tray from the kitchen. And it wasn't for anyone upstairs. I wondered who it was for. So I followed her. And I saw her go through a secret door, hidden in the scullery. I can show you, if you like?'

'No, Janty!' mumbled Mrs Scrabs, beginning to come to. 'We'll all be undone!'

Mrs Speckle poked her in the nose with a wooden spoon to shut her up. 'Now you listen here, Sally Scrabs!' she barked. 'It will be better for you if you start squealing. We've got you now and you're found out! What or who are you hiding?'

'Th-they've only been here a few months,' said Mrs Scrabs eventually. 'Ever since Mr D'Anvers was turfed out. When he first kidnapped them, ten years ago, he ordered Tully to kill them, but Tully couldn't do it. Not with the pregnancy and everything.'

'Who, Mrs Scrabs? Who are you talking about?' asked the great detective, his voice trembling.

'Max and Pru Blades, sir,' said the housekeeper, nervously.

Wilma and Kite gasped. 'They're alive!' the acting headmistress exclaimed.

'And the extra food delivery DID mean something!' Wilma added.

'Take us to them immediately, Mrs Scrabs,' said Theodore, trying to keep his voice steady. 'And you'd better tell us everything on the way.'

'For years we had them imprisoned on the outcrop behind Rascal Rock,' began Mrs Scrabs, as she was dragged to her feet. 'It can't be seen from the mainland.'

'A hidden outcrop? Good Lord!' said Theodore, running a hand desperately through his hair. 'That explains why

I couldn't find them at Rascal Rock. They were never here!'

'But it was a bother keeping them there,' continued Mrs Scrabs, as she led them on. 'Every week Tully had to row me out, winch me up on the rope. It was a right chore keeping them alive. Especially when the baby came . . .'

Wilma gulped. Was Mrs Scrabs talking about her? Kite took Wilma's hand and gently squeezed it reassuringly.

'A draughty outcrop was no place for a child. So we had to get rid of it. They begged us to take her somewhere safe, so out of guilt I brought her to Rascal Rock, but Mr D'Anvers found her. I told him she was my just-dead sister's baby so he wouldn't kill the child, but he still sent her away. He took the baby off to the Twelve Rats' Tails and gave the innkeeper orders to deal with her. When I got wind on the criminal grapevine that he'd packed her off to the Institute, well, the guilt was still bothering me . . . I've been skimming a monthly groggle off Mr D'Anvers food bill ever since, and sending it on to the Institute for the child's upkeep.'

'So in a weird way it was *Barbu D'Anvers* paying for me at the Institute?' Wilma wondered aloud. 'At least he's definitely not my father,' she added gleefully.

Mrs Scrabs froze. 'You? Are you the baby?' She reached out to touch Wilma's face fleetingly before snatching her hand back.

'Well. Well I never . . .' she said, shaking her head a little in disbelief.

'Please carry on,' insisted Theodore urgently.

'Well,' continued Mrs Scrabs, pulling herself together and making her way further down the corridor. 'He thought you were my niece. So that's why he did it. Anything not to have the constant crying, he said. Anyways, as soon as Mr D'Anvers was moved out of Rascal Rock, I moved Max and Pru inside. It meant less walking and climbing for me for a start. But now Mr D'Anvers is back, I'm having to keep them down in the dungeons so he doesn't find out. If he discovers they're still alive, he'll have me and Tully dead in no time.'

'Oh my goodness, Theodore,' said Kite, her eyes full of hope. 'They're here. They're really here!'

'The scullery's right at the end of that corridor,' Mrs Scrabs explained, pointing down a dark-looking tunnel to her left. 'The secret door is camouflaged as a chalkboard. And here's the key.'

Theodore looked across at Kite and then down at his young charge. Wilma's face was filled with a mixture of excitement and terror. 'Wilma,' he said gently, 'I want you to stay right behind me.'

Wilma nodded and, as he turned, her little hands involuntarily went up to grip the back of his coat belt.

'Right,' declared Theodore, filled with determination. 'Lead the way.'

The walls of the corridor behind the secret door were damp and slimy, and as they felt their way slowly Wilma held on tightly to the back of Theodore's coat, not just because it was slippery underfoot, but because she was filled with conflicting emotions and clinging to him made her feel safe. Her mind was a storm of thoughts. Could it be, after all this waiting, she was really about to meet her parents? It was almost too much to bear.

'Look,' she heard Kite call out ahead of her. 'An underground stream next to the pathway. That must be how they got the message in the bottle out. Looks like we've found our damp underground place, Wilma.'

Theodore cast a look down at her over his shoulder. 'How are you doing?' he asked softly.

Wilma looked up at him and mustered a small smile. The sound of running water filled her ears, and as they came to the bottom of the staircase she could see the dark gulley that ran parallel to the passageway. The smell of sea salt burned her nostrils, and so intense was her longing to know what lay ahead that she almost couldn't bear to see where they were going, and she buried herself as near to Theodore's back as she could.

'There!' cried Kite, seeing an orange light glimmering at the end of the passageway. 'There's light coming from under that door. That must be it.'

Wilma's hands were shaking, her heart thumping so loudly she could feel it pumping through her ears.

Kite had reached a large iron door with a grille towards the top of it. She stopped, gave one expectant look towards the others and slid the grille to one side. Wilma heard a man's voice call out, 'Late today, Mrs Scrabs. Any chance of a bit of meat? Pru's very weak.'

Kite clasped a hand to her mouth, tears filled her eyes and, laughing, she called out: 'Max! Pru! We've found you!'

Wilma heard cries of joy and disbelief and peered out from behind Theodore to see two sets of hands thrusting out from the window. They were holding Kite's face.

Kite, wiping the tears from her cheeks and beaming with joy, yelled out. 'It's them! They're here, Theodore! They're really here!' She fiddled with the key in the lock, desperately trying to get the door open.

At last it swung open.

'My dear, dear friends,' said Theodore, walking forward, his voice filled with emotion. And before Wilma could process any of it she felt herself being dragged into a dark cell. She looked up and saw arms embracing her mentor. She buried herself deeper into his back and clamped her eyes shut. She didn't know what to do. She felt utterly overwhelmed.

There were tears; there was laughter.

Max kept saying over and over again, 'I knew you would come. I never doubted it for a minute. Never, Theodore. Not once. My greatest friend. You have found us at last.'

And then, as the laughter subsided, Wilma heard Pru, her voice soft and gentle. She saw her arm come about and clasp Mr G's hand tightly. 'Theodore,' she said, careful and compassionate, 'Betty didn't make it.'

And, suddenly, a terrible sadness filled the room. Wilma felt Theodore's grief shoot through her as she held on to him tighter.

Pru squeezed Theodore's hand. 'I'm so, so sorry,' she whispered.

Theodore said nothing, but Wilma felt his chest rise, filled with emotion. And then he stood a little taller and she felt his arm come about and pull her forward.

'Who's this?' Wilma heard Pru ask, and at that moment Wilma lifted her head and opened her eyes, looking up into the face of the woman she believed to be her mother.

Pru seemed tired, dark rings under her eyes and her cheeks thin and gaunt, but underneath the years of suffering there was an expression so kind and gentle that it filled Wilma with a sorrow that she had been denied it thus far. To Pru's left was Max. His face was half masked by a beard, but sharp, blue eyes were staring down at her with amazement.

'My goodness,' he said. 'Is this who I think it is? How . . . ? But it is. It's her, Pru. It's her.'

Pru knelt down breathlessly and took Wilma's hands. 'This is the second time I've held you,' she whispered. 'The last time was when you were a baby.' And, with a gasp, she enveloped Wilma in her arms and held on as tightly as she could. Wilma screwed her eyes shut as the tears began to tumble. This was the moment she had been waiting for all her life.

She pulled away and, wiping her face, looked up at them both with wide eyes. 'Is it true?' she gulped. 'Are you really my mum and dad?'

Pru blinked and cast a look at Max. They both seemed taken aback.

'Oh my,' said Max, 'you don't know. Do none of you know?'

Know what? KNOW WHAT? Come on! We've only been waiting four whole books for this. GET ON WITH IT.

266

Chapter 31

Pru took hold of Wilma's hand again. 'Come and sit here with me.' She gestured towards a narrow bed against the wall. 'And Max will explain everything.'

'You probably know by now why we disappeared,' Max began, shooting a look towards Theodore. 'We had decided that the only way to discover what had happened to Betty, Theodore's young bride, was to go undercover as a pair of Criminal Elements. Theodore was blaming himself, convinced her kidnapping was because he was about to close the net on his first big case.'

'The Case of the Ginormous Theft,' said Wilma, fingering her Clue Ring.

'That's the one,' said Max, nodding. 'Barbu D'Anvers was just a petty criminal at the time. He was yet to make it big as a villain, but a chance discovery had led to him becoming one of the prime suspects. Theodore was convinced Barbu was behind it all, but just as he was gathering the evidence he needed Betty went missing. Theodore, understandably, was distracted and he was never able to solve the crime.'

'I have no doubt in my mind that Barbu D'Anvers was the mastermind behind the theft,' explained Theodore. 'Immediately after it, Barbu was suddenly able to buy Rascal Rock, but without proof nothing could be done. I allowed him to slip through my fingers. Something I have regretted ever since. I was also convinced that Barbu, knowing I was on to him, had kidnapped Betty so that my investigation would be put on hold. As you know, I had Rascal Rock searched, but to no avail. I confronted Barbu, who, of course, denied everything. And we have been sworn enemies ever since.'

'Our plan,' said Max, taking up the story again, 'was to infiltrate Barbu's inner circle and see if we could find out anything about Betty's location. It took us months just to be able to get anywhere near him, but eventually we began to be trusted by those close to him and that was when we heard about the outcrop.'

Pru's head fell on to her chest. 'That awful place,' she whispered.

'Betty was being held in a cave at the top of the granite tower behind Rascal Rock. She was weak and undernourished, but she was alive . . .' Pru's voice faded and she turned her face away.

'We were very unlucky,' explained Max. 'Unbeknownst to us, Barbu had become suspicious and had had us followed. Before we could get Betty away, we were discovered and imprisoned with her. Then Barbu charged his top henchman, Tully, with getting rid of us. But the pregnancy made him uncomfortable and Mrs Scrabs took pity on us. It was her who kept us alive and talked Tully into her plan. It was a hard existence. But we managed to make the best of it. We were able to keep dry, occasionally light a fire. But then the baby . . . you . . .' said Max, gesturing towards Wilma, 'were born. And things changed.'

Wilma felt Pru's hand tighten about her own.

'So you are my mum,' said Wilma, blinking.

'No, Wilma,' said Pru, gently. '*Betty* was your mum.'

There was a sharp intake of breath from everyone in the room. Wilma's eyes widened, her mouth fell open. 'B-but,' she stammered. 'That means . . .'

But, before she could say another word, Theodore had scooped her into his arms. 'I don't know who's more pleased,' he whispered. 'You or me.'

'Me probably,' laughed Wilma, tears pouring down her cheeks. She buried her face deep into Theodore's shoulder. He was her dad. It simply wasn't possible for her heart to be any fuller.

*

Let's take a pause. If you're being read to by an adult, tell them to go and make themselves a cup of tea. Now lie back, put your hands behind your head and stare upward with the calm satisfaction that you, yes YOU, know *exactly* who Wilma Tenderfoot really is. She's the daughter of Theodore P. Goodman. Wow. Doesn't that feel *good*? But let's not rest on our laurels. We've still got a lot to get through. Buckle up, everyone. And let's crack on to the end.

'The birth had been difficult,' Max continued, laying a hand on Theodore's shoulder. 'And Betty never really recovered. She fell ill soon afterwards, and within days we lost her. Our first priority was to save your child, Theodore, and so we persuaded Mrs Scrabs to take her. And the rest you probably know.'

Theodore nodded solemnly at Max and held Wilma out in front of him. 'How could I not have realized?' he said, beaming. 'The likeness is remarkable. You look just like your mother, Wilma. The blonde hair, the green eyes.'

'And determined,' chipped in Inspector Lemone, wiping the tears from his eyes with the end of his coat sleeve, 'just like her father.'

There was so much to be sad about – Pickle was dead; Wilma had lost the mother she'd never known; Mr Goodman's final hopes of seeing the love of his life were dashed completely –

and Barbu D'Anvers was to blame for it all. And yet Wilma had never been so happy in her life. She was Theodore P. Goodman's daughter. It was amazing.

'I think it's about time we taught Barbu D'Anvers a lesson once and for all,' she said, looking more determined than ever. 'Holding people hostage against their will is precisely the sort of criminal activity we came looking for. Let's finish what we came to do. Are you strong enough to come with us?' she asked, looking at Max and Pru.

'We've waited over ten years for this day,' smiled Pru, as Max draped his arm around her. 'We wouldn't miss it for the world.'

'Then let's end it,' said Wilma, standing tall and looking up at her father. 'Together.'

Are you cheering? You SHOULD BE.

Chapter 32

Barbu threw back his head and screamed. 'MORE things to sign?' he wailed, as Melba lifted yet another stack of papers on to the desk in front of him. 'But it's so BORING.'

'Just a few more signatures required, Cooperate D'Anvers,' said Melba, pulling the top sheet down and placing it in front of him. 'Not long now. And then we'll be done forever.'

But at that moment Theodore burst through the double doors into the throne room. 'I think Mr D'Anvers is done now!'

Barbu shifted sideways so that he could see from behind the tall stack of papers. 'Tully! Guards! Seize them. How they've even managed to get in here is quite beyond me. And how many times do I have to tell you, Goodman? YOU'RE FIRED!'

Captain Brock and his team, seeing Tully and the two henchmen advancing towards Theodore and the others, stepped forward and drew their swords. 'Not another step, gentlemen,' the captain growled, brandishing his weapon.

Barbu frowned. 'Hang on a minute,' he said, concentrating his gaze on Max and Pru. 'Don't I know you two from somewhere? Aren't you supposed to be dead? Tully! Why are they not dead?'

'The thing is, Mr Barbu,' began Tully, gulping, 'I sort of never got round to doing it.'

'IDIOT!' snapped the villain, standing up. 'Anyway, what is this? What do you all want?'

'Your resignation,' said Theodore, his jaw set firm. 'You have been holding Max and Pru against their will. Even if you didn't know it. That's kidnapping. And according to Cooper regulations, because you are currently breaking a law, you are no longer eligible to be the island's Cooperate General.'

'Rubbish!' guffawed Barbu, throwing his head back and laughing. 'The desperate ideas of a desperate man!'

'Actually,' interjected Melba, pulling a thin file from her briefcase, 'Mr Goodman is entirely correct. If a detective discovers that the present Cooperate General is committing a criminal offence, then he or she will be stripped of their office immediately.'

'Ha!' laughed Barbu again triumphantly. 'Then you fail. Seemingly, you all have the memory spans of midges, because

273

Mr Goodman IS NOT A DETECTIVE. Therefore, he can discover nothing!'

'He may not be a detective,' said Wilma, stepping out from behind her father, 'but I am! You've been found out, Barbu D'Anvers. Your rottenness and wickedness ends today.'

Barbu, incredulous, held out his arms. 'Is this some sort of elaborate joke? Am I being hauled from office by a scrawny, badly dressed ten-year-old GIRL? I mean, REALLY?'

'Yes,' said Wilma, pushing her shoulders back. 'REALLY. Miss Toest. Do the official bit.'

'With pleasure,' smiled Melba, pulling out a black scroll and unrolling it. 'Barbu D'Anvers. Your wrongdoing has been revealed. In accordance with Cooper Law you are stripped of your robes of office!'

Brenda and Glenda Blaize stepped forward and in one deft move removed Barbu's cloak and crown.

'Get OFF!' Barbu screamed. 'This is OUTRAGEOUS!'

'You are discharged from your duties and, by the power vested in me, I pronounce your banishment, effective forthwith.'

'Sorry?' said Barbu, still defiant. 'My banishment?'

'You shall be cast adrift, Mr D'Anvers,' explained Melba, rolling the scroll back up. 'Placed in the Boat of Misery and cast adrift. You are banned from ever returning to

274

Cooper. Captain Brock. Take him.'

Barbu, realizing the game was up, narrowed his eyes and glanced towards a pistol that hung on the wall behind him.

'You'll never take me alive!' he yelled, making a leap for it. 'By which I mean YOU won't be alive!'

But Barbu was still wearing his stilt shoes and, standing too quickly, he stumbled. Janty, seeing his chance to make things right once and for all, sped across from the back of the room where he'd been lurking and leaped at the pistol before Barbu could reach it. Panting, he stood with the barrel of the gun fixed on Barbu's face.

'You won't get away with it this time, Mr D'Anvers,' the boy yelled, his face filled with loathing. 'You killed my father. And you killed Pickle. And now you're going to pay. Oh. And by the way. You're REALLY short.'

Barbu's eyes flashed with rage and as Captain Brock handcuffed him and dragged him from the room the beaten villain yelled, 'Mark my words! You have not heard the last of Barbu D'Anvers!'

'That's what they all say,' said Theodore, his moustache twitching.

'What about Tully?' asked Wilma, gesturing to the large henchman who was standing looking sheepish in the corner.

'After all, he did leave Max and Pru alive.'

'Oh,' said Theodore, 'I don't think Cooper has anything to fear from him.'

Wilma glanced over at Janty. He had been victorious and yet he still looked a little miserable.

'Janty,' she said quietly, 'thank you. We couldn't have done this without you.'

'Without even realizing it, Wilma told me about the beautiful father-and-son tableau you secretly carved into the tombola replica, Janty,' said Theodore. 'Your father would have been proud of you today.'

Janty stared at his feet. 'I'm just sorry I couldn't have done it sooner. Then maybe Pickle would still be here.'

Wilma laid a forgiving hand on Janty's forearm.

'Now then,' interrupted Theodore. 'What are we going to do with you, young man? You have no employment, nowhere to go.'

'Well, I was thinking,' said Inspector Lemone, 'would you like to come and be my apprentice? Things have turned out rather well for Goodman since he got one. Thought having an apprentice myself might do the same for me. There's lots of biscuits. One of the perks of the jobs.'

Janty looked stunned. 'Really?' he said. 'I'm not going to be locked up for all the bad things I've done?'

'Oh,' said Theodore, 'I don't think that will serve any purpose. I always say everyone needs a second chance and you've certainly earned yours today.'

'Then, yes, please,' said Janty, nodding. 'I'd very much like to be your apprentice, Inspector Lemone.'

'Excellent!' beamed Lemone, tapping his belly. 'I'd give you a biscuit, but we had to throw everything we had at a grubby fellow in the tunnel. Bad business. Very bad business.'

'So now that Barbu D'Anvers is gone,' said Wilma, frowning a little, 'what's to be done about the island? We've got a load of criminals to get back under control and no one to lead it.'

'I suggest,' said Glenda, 'that we forget this tombola nonsense and ask the people of Cooper who they'd like to lead them. Have candidates stand and tell us what they'd do to help the island and then have everyone vote on it.'

'And Lowsiders too,' said Brenda, 'not just Farsiders.'

'I shall draw up the relevant legal documents and we can put it to the island in the morning,' said Melba.

'Mr Goodman, I mean . . . Dad,' said Wilma, grinning and tugging her father's sleeve, 'I think I'd like it if you were a detective again, please. And I was your apprentice.'

Theodore looked down at his daughter and laughed. 'But you've already been promoted to junior detective, Wilma.

Perhaps we can work together instead? How would you like that?'

'I'd like it very much,' said Wilma, beaming from ear to ear.

You're right. It IS lovely. But we're not quite finished yet. One more chapter to go.

Chapter 33

'Come on, Wilma!' shouted Mrs Speckle up the stairs. 'We're going to be late!'

It had been a few weeks since events had unfolded at Rascal Rock, and a wonderful calm had descended on the island. Melba's suggestion that there be proper elections had been greeted enthusiastically by Farsiders and Lowsiders alike, and, to everyone's delight, Cicatrise Hurl had been elected as the new Cooperate General. His first decree was that the Great Wall that had divided the island for so long be dismantled. Never again would Cooperans be kept apart.

Hearing Mrs Speckle, Wilma ran to her dressing table and took a quick look at herself in the mirror. She had a smudge of something unidentifiable on her cheek, which she rubbed off quickly with the back of her hand, and her pigtails were a little wayward, but other than that she was as spick and span as she'd ever been. Today was a big day and she wanted to look her best.

Clattering down the staircase, she ran into the kitchen where Janty, Inspector Lemone, Mrs Speckle and Theodore were waiting.

'Sorry I'm a bit late,' she panted. 'I was trying to find my hat. But then I remembered I didn't have one. Anyway. I'm ready now.'

'Jolly good,' said Theodore, walking towards the back door and holding it open. 'Then let's be off.'

Spring had finally arrived on the island and, although the air was still crisp and fresh, a hint of warmth was breaking through. Flowers were starting to peep up from the hedgerows and trees were coming into bud. It was as if everything and everyone were shaking off the dark days of winter: new beginnings in more ways than one.

The Central Plaza was packed. At the far end of the square, Wilma could see Cicatrise Hurl, Brenda Blaize next to him and Captain Brock standing at a podium. In front of them a plinth that had been toppled in the uprising was covered in a deep blue velvet cloth and the new United Flag of Cooper was fluttering in the breeze. Following Theodore, Wilma made her way through the crowd. As they went, Farsiders and Lowsiders alike were patting them on the back and thanking them for liberating the island from the mess it had got itself into. Since getting rid of Barbu, Wilma had become quite famous, something she was still having to get used to, but Theodore had taught her how to be polite and gracious, and had made sure all the praise hadn't gone to her head.

'Ah!' called out Brenda, waving. 'You're here! Super. Then we can start the ceremony!' She nodded towards a man holding a long horn at the side of the stage, and seconds later a fanfare filled the air. Wilma climbed up the steps on to the platform and stood next to Theodore, proud and happy to be standing next to her father, the great and serious detective.

'Citizens of Cooper,' began Cicatrise, turning to address the crowd. 'We are here today to honour not one but several heroes of this island. Only a few weeks ago, we were living under a cloud of tyranny, our future was bleak, our island doomed. Yet, because of the incredible bravery of a few, we are all now free. It gives me great pleasure to honour Captain Brock, leader of the 2nd Hawks Brigade, who led the small diversionary force, in which my fiancée, Brenda, was lucky to play a small part, through enemy territory to Rascal Rock. His bravery and his laser-sharp vision saved the day. And so I am delighted to promote Captain Brock to the rank of major.'

Applause and whistles rang out as Captain Brock stepped

forward and received his extra stripes. With one sharp salute, he accepted his new insignia and, giving the crowd a rare smile, took his place next to Theodore.

'And now,' Cicatrise continued, 'there are two other people whom we must honour. Firstly, the incredible Wilma Tenderfoot, who led her team through a labyrinth of underground tunnels straight into the heart of Rascal Rock. Once there the daring gang set free those who had been held hostage and removed those who should never have been in power from their position. To Wilma Tenderfoot, for her bravery and determination, we award the island's greatest honour – the Order of the Cooperan!'

Wilma's eyes popped as wide as they could go. She looked out at the crowd, who were all cheering and waving, and then up at her father.

'Go on then, Wilma,' said Theodore, with a smile. 'Collect your award. You deserve it.'

In a half-daze Wilma stepped forward. Brenda took her hand and shook it firmly, before pinning a small golden outline of the island to her chest. It was the proudest moment of Wilma's life.

'And, finally, there is one more who must be honoured today,' continued Cicatrise. 'Someone else who will be forever remembered. Someone who was steadfast and true and will stand as an example to future generations of what it is to be courageous and loyal. Wilma, perhaps you could do the honours?'

Brenda passed the end of a thick golden rope into Wilma's hand and, bending down, whispered, 'Give that a pull. Make it a good strong one.'

Wilma, who had no idea what was going on, looked down at the plushly tassled rope in her hand. She blinked and looked back up. The crowd in the square had fallen quiet and all eyes were upon her. Screwing her mouth sideways, she tugged on the rope with all her might and suddenly, in front of her, the deep blue cloth above the plinth fell to the floor. Wilma gasped and tears sprang to her eyes. There, standing on a column set into the plinth in the middle of Central Plaza, was a golden statue of Pickle.

'I made him,' a voice whispered in her ear. She looked over to see Janty, who had come up on to the stage, smiling at her. 'I hope you like it.'

Wilma smiled back, tears in her eyes, and, leaning over, kissed him on the cheek. They both stared at each other and blushed. And with that the greatest roar imaginable went up from the crowd.

The celebrations continued way into the afternoon. Sounds of street parties filled the air and everyone was dancing and laughing. Wilma wandered around in a daze, filled with a warm glow that she had never experienced before.

'Can I borrow you for half an hour?' asked Theodore later, interrupting a game of Lantha with Janty. 'You don't mind, do you? Perhaps Inspector Lemone can finish off the game for you.'

'I think Inspector Lemone's a little tied up right now,' said Janty, nodding in the direction of the grinning inspector, who was guiding his new fiancée, Mrs Speckle, proudly around the festivities, arm in arm.

'I'll do it!' said Kite, taking Wilma's seat. 'I don't know the rules, but I expect you can teach me.' Pru and Max sat down beside her to watch.

'Where are we going? Is it a new case? Is trouble brewing?' Wilma asked hopefully, hurrying after her father.

'Nothing like that,' said Theodore, hands behind his back as they walked. 'I'm taking you somewhere to get something. And, no, I'm not telling you what. You'll have to wait and see.'

'Dad,' said Wilma, skipping along to keep up. 'Can I ask you a question?'

'Certainly,' replied Theodore. 'Fire away.'

'What does the P stand for? In Theodore P. Goodman. You've never told me.'

'Oh,' said the great detective, his moustache twitching nervously. 'If I tell you, you have to promise never to repeat it to another soul. Do you swear, Wilma? Nobody else. Understood?'

Wilma made the sign of a cross on her chest. 'Cross my heart and hope to die,' she said solemnly, looking as serious as she knew how.

'Well, all right then,' answered Theodore, coming to a stop just in front of a white picket fence. He looked Wilma squarely in the eye and said, 'The P is for Penelope. It was an accident. Let's never talk of it again.' He cleared his throat and walked on.

'I'll be honest,' said Wilma, hot on his heels. 'I wasn't expecting that.'

'Now then,' said Theodore, his cheeks reddening a little. 'We're here. You wait there,' he added, opening the gate into a beautifully kept garden. 'And I'll go in and have a chat with the owner.'

Wilma nodded and watched as Theodore went round the side of the house to the front door. Then she stared up at the sky and watched as one small cloud meandered its way across the great expanse of blue.

'I wonder where you're going,' she mumbled to herself and then, without thinking, she pursed her lips together and began to whistle. As she was still gazing skyward, she felt something nudge at her ankles. She looked down and there, staring up at her, was a small beagle puppy. 'Hello,' Wilma said, smiling. 'Who are you?'

285

The little thing, who had large brown ears and oversized paws, jumped up and gave two small excited yelps. 'You can smell the biscuit in my pinafore pocket, can't you?' said Wilma, reaching in to break a bit off. 'There you go,' she said. 'Pickle always loved corn crumbles. I expect you do too.'

The puppy gently took the small biscuit morsel from Wilma's fingers and chomped it down gleefully. It wagged its tail and grinned at Wilma, tongue lolling out and panting.

'Wilma!' called Theodore's voice. 'Come and meet Mrs Balding. She owns this Puppy Emporium!'

'Puppy Emporium!' Wilma gasped. 'But that means . . .' She bent down and gave the puppy a stroke. As she did, she saw a little tag about the puppy's neck. It read:

Wilma paused. 'Actually,' she added, picking the puppy up and taking a closer look at her. 'It just so happens I'm in need of an apprentice right now. Would you like to come with me? I think I'll call you Poppy. Like the flowers I saw when I first came to the Farside.'

The puppy pawed Wilma's nose and made a loud fart.

'Good, well that settles it. We'll start your training later,' she added, lowering the puppy to the floor and wafting a hand in front of her nose. 'So I suppose I should introduce myself. My name's Wilma Tenderfoot. I'm a junior detective and nothing and nobody stops me.'

And, with that, she wandered off towards the sound of Theodore's voice, with the little puppy trotting along after her.

And that, dearest reader, is the end of our story. The tale of Wilma Tenderfoot is concluded. Our heroine has triumphed and all is well with the world. And if you learn one thing from Wilma's adventures, let it be this – you may be small, but you can ALWAYS be determined.

THE END

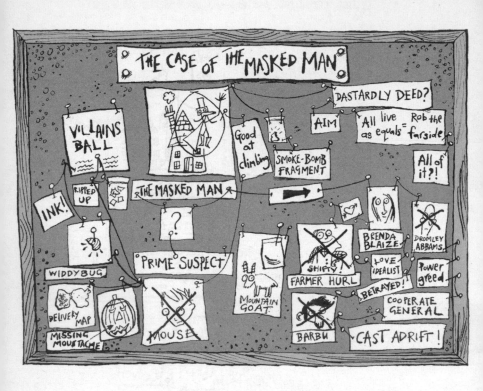

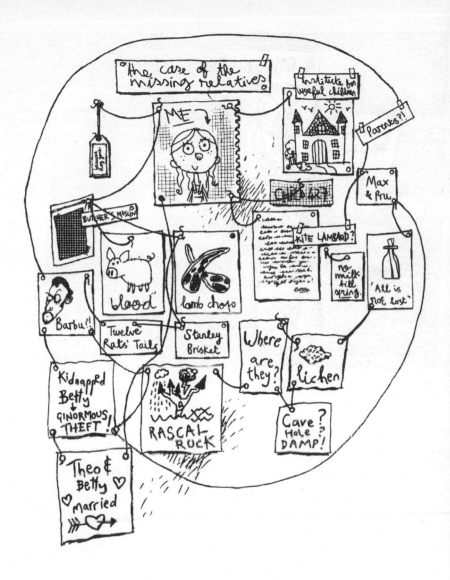

Pickle's Lament

Music by Grace Carey

The Cooper Nod

Music by Charlie Curtis

Wilma Tenderfoot

and the case of the Frozen Hearts

Emma Kennedy

A stolen jewel.
A fish scale.
Some frozen hearts.

Sounds like a case for

Wilma Tenderfoot

Wilma Tenderfoot dreams of one day becoming assistant to the world-famous and very serious detective Theodore P. Goodman. But the last thing Mr Goodman wants is a small and slightly accident-prone sidekick — especially one with an over-friendly beagle called Pickle who keeps eating all the clues.

Still, she's not about to give up — Wilma Tenderfoot may be small but she's very determined.

Wilma Tenderfoot

and the case of
the Putrid Poison

Emma Kennedy

Poisonous foam.
A bucket of seaweed.
Some really bad breath.

Sounds like another case for
Wilma Tenderfoot

Wilma Tenderfoot's dreams have come true – she's official
sidekick to world-famous and very serious detective
Theodore P. Goodman. But with someone snuffing out
stars at the Valiant Theatre, Wilma and her pet dog Pickle
must save the day before the final curtain falls for them all!

A selected list of titles available from Macmillan Children's Books

The prices shown below are correct at the time of going to press. However, Macmillan Publishers reserves the right to show new retail prices on covers, which may differ from those previously advertised.

Emma Kennedy

Wilma Tenderfoot
  of the Frozen He   £5.99

Wilma Tenderfoot
  of the Putrid Poi   £5.99

Wilma Tenderfoo
  of the Fatal Pha   £5.99

All Pan   vebsite,
www.pa   hop and

Bookpos   **IM99 1BQ**

Free postage and packing in the United Kingdom